Henrik J. Krebs

The West-Indian Marine Shells

with some remarks, a manuscript printed for circulation between collectors

Henrik J. Krebs

The West-Indian Marine Shells
with some remarks, a manuscript printed for circulation between collectors

ISBN/EAN: 9783337392178

Printed in Europe, USA, Canada, Australia, Japan

Cover: Foto ©Andreas Hilbeck / pixelio.de

More available books at **www.hansebooks.com**

The West-Indian Marine Shells

with some remarks.

a manuscript printed for circulation between

collectors.

by

1864.

Printed by W. Laubs widow & Chr. Jørgensen, Nykjøbing, Falster.

Index.

	Page.
Acmaea Eschh.	75.
Anomia L.	137.
Aplustrum Schm	92.
Aplysia L.	91.
Arca L.	124.
Artemis Poli	99.
Astralium Link.	82.
Atys Mtf.	94.
Avicula Brug.	131.
Buccinum L.	32.
Bulla L.	92.
Bullia Gray	33.
Bullinula Beck.	92.
Calcar Mtf.	81.
Cancellaria Lmk.	33.
Capsa Brug.	105.
Capulus Mtf.	70.
Cardita Brug.	123.
Cardium L.	115.
Cassis Lmk.	34.
Cerithium Adans.	47.
Chama L.	117.
Chiton L.	89.
Cinulia Gray	71.
Coecum Flem.	75.
Columbella Lmk.	28.
Conopleura Hinds	15.
Conus L.	3.
Corbula Brug.	109.
Crassatella Lmk.	122.
Crepidula Lmk.	69.
Crucibulum Schm.	69.
Cumingia Sowb.	107.
Cyclas Brug.	107.
Cypraea L.	41.
Cypraecassis St.	35.
Daphnella Hinds	9-12.
Delphinula Lmk.	80.
Dentalium L.	91.
Diplodonta Brown	122.

	Page.
Dolium Lmk.	35.
Dreisena Beneden	130.
Eburnea Link.	36.
Emarginula Lmk.	85.
Erato Risso	78. 42.
Eucharis Recl.	111.
Eulima Risso	73.
Euomphalus Sowb.	62.
Fasciolaria Lmk.	15.
Fossarus Adans.	58.
Fimbria M. de M.	122.
Fissurella Brug.	86.
Fusus Brug.	15.
Gastrochaena Sp.	114.
Glauconome Gray	107.
Globulus Schm.	82.
Ianthina Lmk.	65.
Lentilaria Schm.	121.
Lima Brug.	132.
Liotia Gray.	80.
Litiopa Rang.	52.
Littorina Ferr.	58.
Lobiger Krohn.	91.
Lophocercus Krohn.	91.
Lophorus Poli	89.
Lucina Brug.	128, 100-6.
Mactra L.	105.
Magdala Leach.	109.
Magnelia Risso	9-13.
Marginella Lmk.	43.
Melina Retz	132.
Mitra Lmk.	36.
Mitrularia Schm.	69.
Modiolus Lmk.	128.
Modulus Gray	62.
Monostygma Gray	71.
Murex L.	18.
Narica Recl.	68.
Nassa Lmk.	31.
Natica Adans.	66.

Page.

Neaera Gray . . . . 111.
Nerita L. . . . . 76.
Neritina Lmk. . . . . 77.

Odontostoma Flem. . . . . 71.
Oliva Lmk. . . . . 38.
Oniscia Lmk. . . . . 35.
Ostrea L. . . . . 136.
Ovula Brug. . . . . 43.

Patella L. . . . . 88-90.
Pecten O. F. M. . . . . 133.
Pectunculus Lmk. . . . . 126.
Periploma Schm. . . . . 108.
Petricola Lmk. . . . . 108.
Phasionella Lmk. . . . . 79.
Pholadomya Br. . . . . 111.
Pholas L. . . . . 113.
Pinna L. . . . . 130.
Pisania Biv. . . . . 31.
Placunanomia Brod. . . . . 136.
Planaxis Lmk. . . . . 52.
Pleurotoma Lmk. . . . . 7.
Pleurotomaria Def. . . . . 85.
Plicatula Lmk. . . . . 135.
Psammobia Lmk. . . . . 104.
Psammosolea Risso . . . . 113.
Purpura Brug. . . . . 25.
Pyramidella Lmk. . . . . 71.
Pyrula Lmk. . . . . 18.

Ranella Lmk. . . . . 25.
Ricinula Lmk. . . . . 27.
Rissoa Flem. . . . . 53.
Rissoina d'Orb. . . . . 57.

Sanguinolaria Lmk. . . . . 104.
Saxicava Fl. de B. . . . . 107.
Scalaria Lmk. 63
Scrobicularia Schm. . . . . 107.
Semele Schm. . . . . 106.
Semicassis Klein. . . . . 34.
Semiemarginula . . . . 86.
Sigaretus Lmk. . . . . 68.
Siliqvaria Brug. 75

	Page.
Siphonaria Sowb	75.
Solarium Lmk.	62.
Solemya Lmk.	123.
Solen L.	112.
Spondylus L.	135.
Stomatella Lmk.	85.
Stomatia Helb.	85.
Strombus L.	1.
Stylina Flem.	66.
Tellina L.	99.
Terebra Adanson.	33.
Teredo L.	114.
Thracia Leach.	108.
Trapezium M. de M.	123.
Triforis Desh.	51.
Tritonium Cav.	22.
Trochita Risso	72.
Trochus L.	83.
Turbinella Lmk.	16.
Turbo L.	79.
Turbonilla Risso	72.
Turritella Lmk.	46.
Venus L.	95.
Vermetus Adanson	74.
Vitrinella Adams	80.
Volvaria Lmk	46.
Voluta L.	36.
Xenophora F. v. W.	68.

Strombaceæ.

Strombus Linné.

S. accipitrinus Mart. (syn. S. costatus Gml., S. inermis Sowb. Qveen shell, spacy quen-shell). Station: 5 to 7 fathoms water on bluish sand in Spratbay St. Thomas; eats sea-weed; lives in floks. Habitat: — ? Lamarck! West-Indies; Reeve! Antillae; Mörch*)! Haity; D'Orb! Tortola; St. Thomas; St. Croix; Krebs! Guadeloupe; Beau**)! on the authority of C. B. Adams: St. Thomas; J. II. Newton! St. Johns; E. Hartwig! Florida; C. B. Adams! Bermuda; J. Redfield!

S. alatus Gml. (syn. S. pyrulatus. Lamarck, S. pugilis Delw.) Station: — ? — ; habitat: — ? Lamarck! Gulf of Mexico; Reeve! West-Indies & Florida; C. B. Adams! Guadeloupe; Beau! Remark. only a variety of S. pugilis Linné!

S. costoso-muricatus Mart. (syn. S. raninus. Gml., S. affinis Gml., S. curruca Bolt., S. lobatus Sw., S. bitubercularis Lam.). Station: 5 to 7 fathoms water on bluish sand; eats sea-weed; lives in floks tagether with S. accipitrinus. Habitat: l'ocean des Antilles; Lamarck! Antillae; Mörch! Island of Grenada; Reeve! Guadeloupe; Beau! Anguilla; St. Barth; St. Martin; St. Thomas; Trinidad; Barbados; Tortola; Vera-Cruz & Carthagena

---

*) O. A. L. Mørch: catalogus conchyliorum quæ reliquit comes de Yoldi. Hafniæ 1852.

**) M. Beau: catalogue des coquilles recueillies à la Guadeloupe & ses dépendances. Paris 1858.

in N. Gr.; Krebs! and according to C. B. Adams: Tortola; E. Hartwig! Jamaica; C. B. Ad! Carthagena in N. Gr. & Bermuda; J. Redfield!

S. **dubius** Sow. station: — ?; habitat: Jamaica & Florida; C. B. Adams! Jamaica; John C. Jay's Cat. 4te Ed. Remark: not in the collections at St. Thomas.

S. **gallus** L. station: on gravel in 1 to 2 fathoms water. Habitat: Les mers d'Asie & d'Amerique; Lamarck! Antillae; Mörch! Cuba; Martinique; St. Lucy; d'Orb.! the island of St. Johns & at Longpoint on Tortola; Krebs! Guadeloupe; Beau!

S. **gigas** L. King-shell.-station: in 3 to 4 fathoms water on bluish sand; eats species of sphaerococcus (Spaerococcus confervoides Ag.) habitat: Cuba; d'Orb.! Guadeloupe; Beau! Jamaica; C. B. Adams! Bermuda; J. Redfield! St. Thomas; St. Johns; St. Croix; Tortola; St. Barth and Carthagena N. Gr.; Krebs!

S. **Goliath** Chem. station: — ?; habitat: Guadeloupe; Beau! Tortola; Krebs! remark: two specimens from Tortola, but by us until further considered a mere monstrosity of S. gigas Linné. though the two specimens have severel caracters alike, by which they differ from the S. gigas.

S. **granulatus** Sow. Antillae; Mörch!

S. **lentiginosus** L. Cuba; d'Orb.!

S. **pugilis** L. station: two fathoms water on mud-habitat: Gulf of Mexico: Reeve! Cuba: Martinique; Guadeloupe; St. Lucy; Carthagena. N. G.; New-Orleans; d'Orb.! Guadeloupe; Beau! Florida & Jamaica; C. B. Ad! St. Thomas; St. Croix; Tortola; Carthagena in N. G.; Vera-Cruz; Krebs!

Coneae.

Conus Linné.

C. armillatus Ad. station: — ?; habitat: St. Thomas (from Krebs) and Jamaica; C. B. Ad! Remark: we have not seen this species, but we suggest it to be Conus Mindanus Hwass, which C. B. Ad. has described as a new species.

C. aurantius Hwass. station: — ?; habitat: Antillae; Mörch!

C. barbadensis Hwass. station: — ?; habitat: West-Indies; Brugiére! Guadeloupe; Duchassain! Hamsbluff at St. Croix and Just van Dyck's island. near St. Thomas; Krebs! Remark: We do not consider this species to be anything else, than the full grown Conus leucostictus Hwass, which the specimens in our collection fully prove.

C. bacticus Reeve? station: — ?; habitat: Antillae; Mörch!

C. castus Reeve. station: — ?; habitat: St. Thomas; Krebs! Remark: our specimen answers perfectly to the drawing and the description in Reeve's icon. chon., but we do not consider it to be anything else than a young Conus daucus Hwass, which species does not get the impressed lines before they approach the full size.

C. cedo-nulli L. station: in deep water according to Reeve; habitat: West-Indies; Reeve! St. Thomas; St. Croix; Tortola; Krebs!

C. centurio Born. station: — ?; habitat: les mers des Antilles; Lamarck! Island of Margarita; R. Swift! Hamsbluff at St. Croix; Krebs!

C. caracteristicus Chem. station: — ?; habitat:

ocean americaine; Lamarck! West-Indies; Reeve! Re-mark: in none of the collections at St. Thomas.

C. columba Hwass. station: probably in very deep water as Mr. Beau, who is an excellent collector, says: „I never found it without being more or less broken by rolling"; — habitat: common at the island of Marie galante near Guadeloupe; Beau! West-Indies; Reeve! Jamaica; C. B. Ad!

C. cretaceus Knr. station: — ?, habitat: West-Indies; S. Hovey! Jamaica; C. B. Ad!

C. daucus L. station: in very deep water; habitat: Martinique & St. Lucy; de Candé! Hotessier! Guadeloupe; Beau! de Candé! Hotessier! Cuba; de la Sagra! Auber! St. Martin; Tortola; Just van Duck's island near St. Thomas; Krebs! St. Thomas; R. Swift! Jamaica; C. B. Ad!

C. daucus v. luteus together with the orange-coloured species.

C. echinulatus Kien. station: — ?; habitat: Gua-deloupe; Beau!

C. fumigatus Hw. station: — ?; habitat: seas of America (?); Reeve! Lmk.!

C. granulatus L. station: — ?; habitat: Guade-loupe; Beau! Ind. orient; Mörch!

C. leoninus Hw. station: see conus spurius; habitat: Antillae; Mörch! Coast of Mexico & West-Indies; Reeve! Guadeloupe; Beau! Remark: it does not deserve to stand at a species, scarsely as a variety of Conus spurius Gml.; C. leoninus stands as one of the strongest proofs for the eagerness of collectors to increase the numbers in their catalogues; the difference only consisting in the colour.

C. leucostictus Hw. (C. nebulosus Sol.) station: — ?; habitat: Antillae; Mörch! West-Indies; Reeve! Cuba; de la Sagra! Martinique & St. Lucy; de Candé! St. Johns; E. Hartwig! Jamaica; C. B. Ad.! Guadeloupe; Beau! St. Thomas; St. Croix; St. Martin; Trinidad; Krebs!

C. maculiferus Brod. station: — ?; habitat: Guadeloupe; Beau!

C. mercator L. station: on sand; Reeve! habitat: Nevis; by Cap. Power according to Reeve! Antillae; Mörch! one very large, but poor, specimen found at Smithsbay, St. Thomas; Krebs!

C. minutus Reeve. station: — ?; habitat: Island of St. Vincent; Guilding!

C. mindanus Hw. station: at certain seasons, between loose stones close to the shore on 1 to 2 feet water; habitat: Philippines; Lamarck! Reeve! Antillae; Mörch! Curacao; R. Swift! St. Thomas; St. Barth; Anguilla; St. Martin; Krebs! remark: the old, full grown specimens are very different from the young, which have on granulation at all; see Conus pusio.

C. mus Hw. (C. Barbadensis Hw.). station: young shells found in two to three feet water, between stones overgrown with seeweed. habitat: l'ocean des Antilles sur les cotes de la Guadeloupe; Lamarck! Antillae; Mörch! Vera-Cruz; Cuba; St. Lucy; Martinique & Guadeloupe; d'Orb! Jamaica; C. B. Ad! St. Johns; E. Hartwig! St. Thomas; St. Croix; St. Johns; St. Barth; St. Martin; and at St. Martha & Carthagena in Nw. Gr.; Krebs! Arecibo Puertoricco; J. H. Newton!

C. musicus Hw. station: — ?; habitat: West-Indies; by Capt. Power according to Reeve! West-Indies; by S. Hovey according to C. B. Adams!

C. nodiferus Kien. station: — ? —; habitat: Guadeloupe; Beau!

C. puertoricanus Hw. station: — ? —; habitat: Puertoricco; Lamarck! Reeve!

C. punctatus Hw. (C. piperatus Delw., C. biliosus Bolt.) station: — ? —; habitat: Carthagena. New Grenada; according to C. B. Ad! St. Martha in N. Gr.; Krebs!

C. purpurascens Brod. station: — ? —; habitat: Guadeloupe; Beau!

C. pusio Brug. station: — ? —; habitat: Antilles; Lamarck! remark: we consider the name of c. pusio syn. with conus Mindanus; the pusio being described after young specimens, which do not possess the coracters of the full grown shell.

C. spurius Gml. (C. proteus Hw. and according to Beau C. pseudo Thomae Chem.) station: on bluish mud, together with Strombus accipitrinus Mart. in 5 to 7 fathoms water; habitat: l'ocean d'Atlantique et celui d'Amerique; Lamarck! Antillae; Mörch! St. Thomas; Reeve! d'Orb.! St. Johns; E. Hartwig! Guadeloupe; Beau! St. Thomas; St. Croix; St. Johns; Tortola; Krebs!

C. pygmaeus Reeve. station: — ? —; habitat: ? Reeve! Antillae; Mörch! St. Thomas; Tortola; Krebs!

C. radiatus Gml. (C. Martinianus R., C. gubba. Ki. ?). station: — ? —; Antillae? Mörch!

C. roseus Lamarck. station: — ? —; habitat: Les mers des Antilles; Lamarck! West-Indies; Reeve! St. Thomas; Krebs! remark: we consider this a variety of Conus mus Hw.; we possess a specimen which is rose-colored, but they do else correspond in all other respects with C. mus.

C. testudinarius Martini. station: — ? —; habitat West-Indies; Lamarck! Reeve! Guadeloupe; Beau!

C. varius L. (C. granulosus. Bolt.), station: supposed to be in very deep water. Habitat: West-Indies; Surinam; Brasils; Lamarck! Antillae; Mörch! St. Croix; R. Swift! Antigua; Reeve! St. Thomas; Zioch! Krebs! Jamaica; C. B. Adams!

C. verrucosus Hw. (C. granulatus. Mart. non L.) station: — ? — ; habitat: Antillae; Mörch!

C. Villepinii Fish. & Bern. station: — ? — , habitat: Marie Galante; Beau!

Pleurotomaceæ.

Pleurotoma Lamarack.

P. affinis Grays Man. station: — ? , habitat: St. Vincent; Guilding! St. Thomas; Knox! Guadeloupe; Beau!

P. albella Ad. station: — ? — ; habitat: Jamaica; C. B. Adams!

P. albida Ad. station: — ? ; habitat: Jamaica; C. B. Adams!

P. alabaster Reeve. station: — ? — ; habitat: Carthagena in Nw. Gr.; John Redfield according to C. C. Adams!

P. albocincta Ad. station: — ? — ; habitat; St. Thomas; St. Martin & Waterisland; Krebs! Jamaica; C. B. Adams! Guadeloupe; Petit!

P. albomaculata Ad. station: — ? ; habitat: Jamaica; C. B. Ad.!

P. albomaculata d'Orb. Moll. de Cuba, pt. 2 pg. 176 pl. 24 fig. 15—18. station: — ? — ; habitat: Cuba; d'Orb.! Guadeloupe; Beau!

P. angulifera Reeve. station: very deep water, d'Orb.!
habitat: West-Indies; d'Orb.!

P. Antillarum d'Orb. Moll. de Cuba, pt. 2 173 pl. 24
fig. 1—3. station: — ?; habitat: Cuba; Martinique;
d'Orb.! Guadeloupe; Beau!

P. augustae Ad. station: — ? —; habitat: Jamaica;
C. B. Ad.!

P. Auberiana d'Orb. Moll. de Cuba, pt. 2 pg. 174 pl.
24 fig. 4, 6. station: — ? —; habitat: Martinique;
Cuba; d'Orb.! Guadeloupe; Beau!

P. balteata Reeve. station: ?; habitat: St. Thomas;
R. Swift!

P. cancellata Gray. station: — ? —; habitat: St.
Vincent; Guilding! St. Thomas; Krebs!

P. Candeana d'Orb. Moll. de Cuba, pt. 2 pg. 175 pl.
24 fg. 10—12. station: — ? —; habitat: Martinique; Guadeloupe; d'Orb.! Guadeloupe; Beau!

P. candidula Reeve. station: very deep water, d'Orb.!
habitat: West-Indies; d'Orb.!

P. caribaea d'Orb. Moll. de Cuba, pt. 2 pg. 173 pl. 23
fg. 32—34; station: — ? —; habitat: Cuba; Guadeloupe; Martinique; d'Orb.! Guadeloupe; Beau!

P. clathratus Reeve. station: very deep water, d'Orb.;
habitat: West-Indies; d'Orb.!

P. coccinata Reeve. station: — ? —; Saba; R. Swift!
St. Thomas; St. Johns; Crabisland; St. Barth; St. Martin; Anguilla; Krebs! St. Thomas; C. B. Ad.!

P. collaris Reeve. station: — ? —; habitat: Guadeloupe; Beau!

P. costata Gray. station: ?; habitat: Guadeloupe
& Martinique; d'Orb.! Guadeloupe; Beau! St. Vincent;
Reeve! St. Thomas; St. Johns; St. Barth; St. Martin;

Anguilla; Krebs! remark: it is surely synonyme with Pl. trifasciata. Gray; we have specimens withaut lines and specimens with 1 and 2 and 3 lines on the upper whorls.

P. decorata Ad. is a Daphnella.

P. deminuta see Mangelia qvadrata Reeve!

P. d'Orbignii Reeve. station: dredged from deep water d'Orbigny!; in bluish mud in 6 to 8 feet water R. Swift! Knox! habitat: St. Thomas; R. Swift! Knox! Lillienskjold! Krebs!

P. Dorvillae Gray. station: ?; habitat: St. Vincent; Guilding! Guadeloupe; Beau!

P. elatior Ad. station: ?, habitat: Jamaica; C. B. Adams!

P. elatior d'Orb. Moll. de Cuba, pt. 2 pg. 173 pl. 23 fig. 35—37; station: ?; habitat: St. Thomas; de Candé! Guadeloupe; Beau!

P. flavo-cincta Ad. station: — ? —; habitat: Jamaica; C. B. Ad.!

P. fucata Reeve. station: — ? —; habitat: — ? Reeve! Antillae; Mörch! Guadeloupe; Duchassain! St. Thomas; St. Barth; Anguilla; St. Martin; Krebs!

P. fuscescens Gray. station: — ? —, habitat: Mauritius; Kien! Guadeloupe; Beau! St. Thomas; St. Croix; Krebs! Antillae; Mörch! remark: should this not prove to be synonyme with Pleurotoma nigrescens Gray?

P. fusco-cincta Ad. station: — ? —; habitat: Jamaica; C. B. Ad.!

P. fusiformis Ad. station: — ? —; habitat: Jamaica; C. B. Ad.!

P. Guildingii Reeve. station: — ? —; habitat: St.

Vincent; Guilding! St. Thomas (?); Krebs! Guadeloupe; Beau!

P. **harpula** Val. station: — ? — : habitat: New-Holland; Kien! Antillae; Mörch! St. Thomas; R. Swift! John Knox! St. Croix; Krebs! remark: stands very near Pl. fuscescens and Pl. nigrescens Gray and is perhaps synonyme.

P. **hastula** Reeve. station: — - ? — ; habitat: St. Thomas; Krebs!

P **Jayana** Ad. station: — ? — ; habitat: Jamaica; C. B. Ad.! St. Thomas; Krebs! remark: a very doubtful species, likely synonyme with. Pl. zebra Kiener!

P. **Lavelleana** d'Orb., pt. 2 pg. 174 pl. 24 fig. 7, 9. station: — ? — ; habitat: Cuba; Jamaica; Guadeloupe; Martinique; d'Orb.! Guadeloupe; Beau!

P. **lagueata** Reeve. station: in very deep water d'Orb.! habitat: West-Indies; d'Orb.!

P. **luctuosa** d'Orb. station: — ? — ; habitat: Cuba; d'Orb.! pt. 2 pg. 172 pl. 23, fig. 29—31. Guadeloupe; Beau!

P. **maculata** Ad. station: — ? ; habitat: St. Thomas; and Jamaica; C. B. Ad.!

P. **minor** Ad. station: — ? — ; habitat: Jamaica; C. B. Ad.!

P. **monilifera** Sowb. station: — ? — ; habitat: Jamaica; C. B. Ad.!

P. **nigrescens** Ad. station: — ? — ; habitat: Jamaica; C. B. Ad.! remark: is this and the P. semi-granosa Reeve not synonyme?

P. **nigrescens** Gray. station: under flat pieces of madrepores in 1 to 2 feet water; habitat: St. Vincent; Guilding! Guadeloupe; Beau! St. Thomas; St. Croix;

Anguilla; & St. Martin; Krebs! remark: see P. fuscescens Gray & P. harpula Val. & P. semigranosa Reeve.

P. nodata Ad. station: — ? —; habitat: Jamaica; C. B. Ad.!

P. obesicostata Reeve. station: very deep water d'Orb.! habitat: West-Indies; d'Orb.!

P. ornata d'Orb. pt. 2 pg. 171 pl. 23 fig. 26, 28; habitat: Cuba; d'Orb.!

P. pagodus Reeve. station: — ? —; habitat: — ? Reeve! St. Thomas?; Krebs!

P. paria Reeve. station: — ? —; habitat: ? Reeve! St. Thomas; John Knox!

P. pellis-phocae Reeve. station: — ? — ; habitat: — ? Reeve! St. Thomas; R. Swift!

P. paxillus Reeve. station: — ? —; habitat: St. Jan; St. Thomas; Krebs! remark: perhaps synonyme with P. fuscescens Gray, P. harpula Val. and P. nigrescens Gray.

P. pentagonalis Gray. station: — ? — ; habitat: St. Vincent; Guilding! Guadeloupe; Beau!

P. pulchella Reeve. station: — ? —; habitat: — ? Reeve! Antillae; Mörch!

P. pulchra Gray. station: — ? — ; habitat: St. Vincent; Guilding! St. Thomas; Knox! Krebs!

P. pygmaea Ad. station: — ? —; habitat: Jamaica; C. B. Ad.!

P. pura Reeve. station: — ? — ; habitat: St. Martin; Krebs!

P. qvadrifasciata Reeve. station: — ? —; habitat: Jamaica; C. B. Ad.!

P. qvadrilineata Ad. station: — ? — ; habitat: Jamaica; C. B. Ad.! remark: we have not seen authentic specimens of this species, but we are inclined to think it synonyme with P. costata Gray and P. trifasciata Gray.

P. rubicata Reeve. station: very deep water; habitat: West-Indies; d'Orb.!

P. semigranosa Reeve. station: — ? — ; habitat: — ? — ; Reeve! St. Thomas; Krebs! remark: see P. nigrescens. Ad.!

P. solida Ad. station: — ? — ; habitat: Jamaica; C. B. Ad.! West-Indies; S. Hovey!

P. trifasciata Gray. (see P. costata Gray.)

P. turbinelloides Reeve. station: very deep water; habitat: West-Indies; d'Orb.!

P. urnula Reeve (?). station: — ? — ; habitat: St. Thomas; R. Swift!

P. Vespuciana d'Orb. pt. 2 pg. 175 pl. 24 fig. 13, 15. station: — ? — ; habitat: Guadeloupe; Martinique; Cuba; d'Orb.! Guadeloupe; Beau!

P. Virgo Lmk. station: — ? — ; habitat: Cartagena. Nw-Gr., John Redfield, accordding to C. B. Ad.!

P. zebra Lmk. station: — ? — ; habitat: Mauritius; Kiener! Antillac; Mörch! St. Thomas; Knox; St. Thomas; St. Johns; Water-Island; Krebs!

Daphnella Hinds.

D. lymnaciformis Kiener. station: — ? — ; habitat: Philippine Islands; Cuming! Antillac; Mörch! St. Thomas; Bland! Guadeloupe; Duchassain! Beau! Petit! St. Thomas; St. Johns; Jamaica; Ad.! Just van Dyck's Island and Water-Island near St. Thomas; St. Thomas; St. Johns; St. Barth; St. Martin; Anguilla; Krebs! remark: the localities of C. B. Adams refer to Daphnella decorata, described by him; it is certainly synonyme

with D. lymnaeiformis K. from which C. B. Adams,
once in a conversation, acknowledged not to be able to
distinguish it without by the locality; we do not acknow-
ledge this to be a suficient argument to establish species
on and we really regret that such doctrins have been
able to enter, to multiply and to confuse the nomen-
clature and the sciense.

Magnelia Risso.

M antillarum Reeve. station: — ? — ; habitat:
West-Indies; Reeve!

M. angulata Reeve. station: — ? —; habitat: — ? —;
Reeve! remark: we have found a species at St. Thomas, which approaches the drawing in Reeve's Ic. conch.
very much.

M. badia Reeve station: dead specimens between stones
and species of corals in 2 feet water; habitat: — ?
Reeve! St. Thomas; Krebs! remark: see M. crassicostata Ad.!

M. balteata Reeve. station: in mud from 6 to 8 feet
water; habitat: -? —; Reeve! St. Thomas; St. Barth;
St. Martin; Anguilla; Krebs!

M. biconica Ad. station: — ? —; habitat: Jamaica;
C. B. Adams!

M. biconica var. alba Ad. station: — ? —; habitat:
Jamaica; C. B. Adams!

M. brevis Ad. station: — ? — ; habitat: Jamaica;
C. B. Adams!

M. candidissima Ad. station: — ? —; habitat: Jamaica; C. B. Adams! St. Thomas; Bland!

M. crassicostata Ad. station: — ? — ; habitat:

Jamaica; C. B. Ad.! remark: we consider this and M. badia Reeve as synonymes.

M. densestriata Ad. station: — ? — ; habitat: Jamaica; C. B. Adams! remark: we have until further laid this species together with M. baltcata Reeve in our collection.

M. Hornbecki Reeve. station: — ? — ; habitat: St. Thomas; Hornbeck! Krebs! remark: Reeve's drawing of this shell is very bad.

M. lanceolata Ad. station: — ? — ; habitat: Jamaica; C. B. Adams!

M. luteofasciata Reeve. station: — ? — ; habitat: — ? — ; Reeve! St. Thomas; Knox!

M. multilineata Ad. station: — ? — ; habitat: St. Thomas (from Bland); Jamaica; C. B. Ad!

M. muricoides Ad. station: — ? — ; habitat: Jamaica; C. B. Ad.!

M. occidentalis Reeve. station: dredged from very deep water; habitat: West-Indies; Reeve! St. Thomas; Krebs! remark: Pleurotoma occ. Reeve.

M. qvadrata Reeve. station: — ? — ; habitat: — ? — ; Reeve! St. Thomas; R. Swift! Krebs! St. Martin; Krebs! Jamaica; C. B. Adams! remark: it is a Pleurotoma of Reeve and we take it to be synonyme, with C. B. Adams' Pleurotoma deminuta.

M. astricta Reeve. station and habitat: — ? — ; remark: we have found a species at St. Thomas, which approaches the drawing and the description of M. ast. in Reeve's Ic. conch. as much as many shells described and drawn in said work, answer to the descriptions and the drawings intended to represent them.

M. tincta Reeve. station: — ? — ; habitat: St. Thomas; Lillienskjold! remark: Pleurotoma Reeve.

M. triticea Reeve (Pleurotoma). station: — ? — ; habitat: St. Thomas; Knox! Anguilla; received twice from there; Krebs!

Conopleura Hinds.

C. cancellata d'Orb. (Sinusigera). station: — ? — ; habitat: Jamaica; de Candé!

Fusus Bruguiére.

F. distans Lmk. station: — ? — ; habitat: — ? —; Mörch! Philippines; Reeve! Cartagena, Nw. Gr.; John Redfild! Bay of Campechy; C. B. Adams! South-Caroline; Say!

F. gradatus Reeve. station: dredged from 15 fathoms water; habitat: St. Thomas; Krebs!

F. lineatus Chem. (F. ansatus. Gml.). station: — ? —; habitat: Antillae; Mörch!

F. muricoides Ad. station: — ? — ; habitat: Jamaica; C. B. Adams!

F. nitens Ad. station: — ? — ; habitat: Jamaica; C. B. Adams!

F. reuma Mart. station: — ? — ; habitat: Antillae Mörch!

Fasciolaria Lamarck.

F. gigantea d'Orb. station: — ? —; habitat: Cuba; d'Orb.! Moll. de Cuba, pt. 2 pg. 169 pl. 23 fig. 25.

F. Tulipa Lmk. station: on 2 a 6 feet water on sand and small stones, where Algae are growing and where the sea is calm; it is in very large qvantity in the creeks around the town of Carthagena in N. Gr.; habitat: Antillae; Mörch! Guadeloupe; Beau; Cuba; Guade-

loupe; St. Thomas; Columbia; d'Orb.! Honduras; Dyson!
St. Thomas; St. Johns; Tortola; Trinidad; St. Martin;
Carthagena, Nw. Gr.; Krebs! Florida; South-Caroline;
Jamaica; Chagres; C. B. Ad.!

Turbinella Lamarck.

T. ananas Chem. (M. infundibulum. Gml., B. sulcatum
Msch.) station: in deep water, but at certain seasons
between stones close to the shore; habitat: West-
Indies; Reeve! Antillae; Mörch! Martinique; Guadeloupe;
St. Lucy; d'Orb.! Guadeloupe; Beau! Jamaica; C. B.
Adams! St. Martin; St. Croix; St. Thomas; Krebs!

T. annulata Bolt. station: — ? — ; habitat: Antillae; Mörch! St. Johns and Just van Dyck's Island
near St. Thomas; Krebs!

T. attenuata Reeve. station: — ? — ; habitat: — ?
—; Reeve! Antillae; (?) Mörch!

T. brevicaudata Reeve. station: — ? — ; habitat: — ? — ; Reeve! Tortola; St. Thomas; St. Johns;
C. B. Adams! remark: should this not be synonyme
with P. filamentosa Kock?

T. capitellum L. station: — ? — ; habitat: Antillae; Mörch! Martinique; Guadeloupe; St. Lucy; d'Orb.!
Guadeloupe; Beau! St. Thomas; R. Swift! Krebs!

T. carinifera Lmk. station: — ? — ; habitat: St.
Thomas; Krebs!

T. cingulifera Lmk. station: — ? — ; habitat:
Guadeloupe; Beau!

T. filimentosa Koch. station: — ? — ; habitat:
Antillae; Mörch! St. Thomas; Tortola; Krebs!

T. fuscata Gml. (Turbinella angularis Reeve). station:
— ? — ; habitat: Antillae; Mörch!

T. gibbula Gml. (T. filosus Lmk.) station: — ? — ;
habitat: Antillae; Mörch!

T. globulus Lmk. station: — ? — ; habitat: Antigua?; Krebs! remark: Does the figure in Reeve's
Ic. conch. really represent this species?

T. gracilis Reeve. station: — ? — ; habitat: St.
Thomas; Krebs!

T. leucozonalis Lamk. station: — ? — ; habitat:
St. Thomas; St. Croix; Tortola; Krebs! Honduras; Reeve!
Jamaica; Carthagena; Nw. Gr. (acc. to Redfield!) C. B.
Adams!

T. lineata Lmk. station: — ? — ; habitat: St. Thomas; Krebs!

T. muricata Born (T. pugillaris Lmk.) station: — ? — ;
habitat: Antillae; Mörch! Tortola; Krebs! Martinique;
d'Orb.! Guadeloupe; Beau! St. Johns; Jamaica; C. B.
Adams!

T. nana Reeve. station: — ? — ; habitat: St. Thomas
& St. Croix; Krebs!

T. nassa Gml. station: — ? — ; habitat: Cuba; St.
Lucy; Martinique; Guadeloupe; St. Thomas; d'Orb.!
Jamaica; St. Thomas; C. B. Adams!

T. nigella Chem. (P. ocellata Gml.) station: — ? — ;
habitat: Antillae; Mörch! Guadeloupe; Beau! St. Thomas; Anguilla; St. Martin; Krebs!

T. polygona Lmk. station: — ? — ; habitat: Cuba;
Bahia; d'Orb.!

T. recurvirostra Wagn. station: — ? — ; habitat:
Philippines; Reeve! Antillae; Mörch!

T. rhinoceros Lmk. station: — ? — ; habitat: Zan-
zibar; Reeve! Carthagena; Nw. Gr. (according to J.
Redfield); C. B. Adams!

T. rudis Reeve. station: — ? —; habitat: St. Thomas; St. Johns and Guadeloupe; Krebs!

Pyrula Lamarck.

P. aruana L. (P. carica Gml.) station: —? —; habitat: Antillae; Mörch!

P. melongena L. station: —?—; habitat: Antillae; Mörch! Cuba; Martinique; Guadeloupe; Carthagena N. Gr.; Florida; d'Orb.! Guadeloupe; Beau! Carthagena New-Gr.; Redfield! Jamaica; C. B. Adams! St. Juan de Nicaragua; Tortola; Krebs!

P. morio L. (Fusus coronatus Lmk.) station: on mud; habitat: Brasils; Martinique; Cuba; d'Orb.! Trinidad; Reeve! Guadeloupe; Beau! Duchassin!

P. perversa Lmk. station: — ? — ; habitat: Cuba; Mississippi; d'Orb.!

Murex Linné.

M. alveatus Kien. station: on 1 or 2 feet water, between pieces of Madrepores; habitat: Antillae; Mörch! Jamaica; C. B. Adams! Guadeloupe; Beau! St. Thomas; St. Croix; St. Martin; Krebs!

M. Beauii Fisch. & Bern. station: — ? — ; habitat: Marie Galante; Beau!

M. bellus Reeve. station: a dead specimen dredged from 10 fathoms water on bluish mud; habitat: Antillae?; Mörch! Tortola; A. H. Riise! St. Thomas; Krebs!

M. bilineatus Reeve. station: — ? — ; habitat: Goyave; Beau!

M. brevifrons Lmk. (M. calcitrapa Lmk.) station: — ? — ; habitat: Antillae; Mörch! Martinique; Guadeloupe; Cuba; St. Thomas; Brasils; d'Orb.! Jamaica; Carthagena

Nw. Gr.; C. B. Adams! remark: this will surely later prove identical with Murex cornu cervi Martini.

M. Cailleti Petit. station: — ? — ; habitat: Guadeloupe; Beau!

M. cancellatus Sowb. station: — ? — ; habitat: St. Johns; Knox!

M. chrysostoma Gray. station: — ? — ; habitat: Island of Margarita; Mörch! R. Swift!

M. cornu-cervi Mart. (M. breviforns Lmk., M. calcitrapa Lmk., M. purpuratus Reeve) station: on stinking bluish mud 10 to 12 feet below the surface of the water in a creek with smooth water depositing eggs; habitat: Antillae; Mörch! Guadeloupe; Beau! St. Thomas; Krebs! remark: we possess specimens, which have been taken out of the eggs and every step of development until the size of Murex purpuratus Reeve, drawn in his Ic. conch. and they fully prove the synonymes mentioned above, to be correct. It is proper to remark: that some specimens have one and others have two nodules between each varix, although taken out of one cluster of eggs, but all the old and full-grown specimens have only one nodule, some with a very faint indication of the second, between each varix, young specimens have no sculpture before on the fourth or fifth whorl.

M. crassivaricosa Reeve. station: — ? — ; habitat: Guadeloupe; Beau! St. Thomas; Krebs! remark: we have laid four specimens, with this name, in our collection, but we are inclined to think that the Murex crassivaricosa Reeve is only a Murex carnu-cervi Mart.

M. elegans Bech. station: — ? — ; habitat: St. Domingo; St. Martin; d'Orb.! Port-Louise in the island of Fajau near Guadeloupe; Beau! remark: Beau says:

„it is only found at certain seasons". It is a very re-
marcable fact how common certain species of marine-
shells appear at certain localities for a lenght of time
and thereafter disappear for many years; perhaps some
species, which are living in the deepest parts of the sea,
come, at certain seasons, to the shores to breed; Rvd.
Ziock has at least once found 6 or 8 full-grown life
specimens of Turbinella ananas Chem. on one to two
feet water, close to the shore; Reeve says that the Turbinella ananas Chem. lives in deep water and we have
never found it close to the shore, thaugh we in 17 years
have made excursions around the W. Ind - Islands; we
have likewise once found several specimens of Murex
hexagonus Lmk. in one place close to the shore and
since than not found it for many years.

M. elongatus Lmk. station: — ? — ; habitat: Gulf
of Mexico; Reeve! remark: Perhaps a variety of
Murex cornu-cervi Mart; Reeve makes the same mistake
by the drawing of this species as by Nr. 5, 13, 14,
20, 23, 24. 25 and many more in the Ic. conch. in re-
presenting young specimens, where the characteristic
enameled lip is not yet eveloped.

M. funiculatus Reeve. station: on stones in one or
two feet water in the creeks around Carthagena; habitat: Jamaica; C. B. Adams! Carthagena in New-Granada; Krebs!

M. hexagonus Lmk. station: young specimens found at
St. Thomas between pieces of corals and stones on 1 to
2 feet water; habitat: Antillae; Mörch! Guadeloupe;
Bean! St. Thomas; St. Johns; Jamaica; C. B. Adams!
St. Thomas; Tortola; Krebs! remark: we found this
shell quite commonly at the shores of St. Thomas in

1851—52; it has been rare before and since that period.

M. intermedius Ad. (M. alveatus. Kiener).

M. megacerus Sowb. station: — ? — ; habitat: West-Indies; Reeve! Guadeloupe; Beau!

M. Messorius Sowb. station: on stones in 1 or 2 feet water; habitat: — ? Reeve! Jamaica; C. B. Adams! Martinique; de Candé! Guadeloupe; Beau!

M. motacilla Chem. station: — ? — ; habitat: Senegal; Reeve! Guadeloupe; Beau!

M. nodatus Reeve. station: — ? — ; habitat: Guadeloupe; Beau!

M. nuceus Mörch. station: at St. Thomas, under stones and pieces of Modrepores on one or two feet water; habitat: Antillae; Mörch! St. Croix; St. Thomas; St. Martin; Krebs!

M. oculatus Reeve. station: — ? — ; habitat: Jamaica; C. B. Adams! We do not know this species, but it seems to stand Murex pomiformis Mart. very near.

M. pleurotomoides Reeve. station: — ? — ; habitat: St. Martin; Krebs!

M. pauperculus Ad. (Triton Cantrainei Reel.) station: between rocks and pieces of corals on 1 to 2 feet water; habitat: Jamaica; C. B. Adams! Guadeloupe; Beau! St. Thomas; St. Johns; Krebs!

M. pomiformis Mart. station: on coral-reefs; Reeve! dredged from four fathoms water, on bluish sandy mud and on sand in 3 to 4 feet water between sea-weed, where it feeds on Lucina pensylvanica; habitat: Antillae; Mörch! Rio-Janeiro; Martinique; Guadeloupe; St. Thomas; d'Orb.! St. Vincent; Guilding! Jamaica; C. B. Adams! St. Thomas; Tortola; St. Martin; Carupano in Venezuela; remark: young specimens have two and three nodules between each varix, but the full-grown specimens have only one nodule between each varix.

M. pudicus Reeve. station: — ? — ; habitat: Island of Domingo; Reeve!

M. pudoricolor Reeve. station: St. Thomas on a few feet water between stones; Knox! habitat: St. Thomas; Robert Swift! Guadeloupe; Beau!

M. purpuratus Reeve. see M. cornu-cervi Mart.

M. rarispina Lmk. station: — ? — ; habitat: St. Domingo; Lmk! Jamaica; C. B. Adams!

M. rubidentatus Reeve. station: — ? — ; Guadeloupe; Duchassain! Beau!

M. spectrum Reeve. station: — ? — ; habitat: Guadeloupe; Beau!

M. similis Sowb. station: — ? — ; habitat: Guadeloupe; Beau! Duchassain!

M. trigonulus Lmk. station: — ? — ; Marie Galante; Terre-de-Bas des Saintes; Beau!

M. tetragonus? Brod. (M. breviculus Sow.) station: — ? — ; habitat: Guadeloupe; Beau!

Tritonium Cuvier.

T. americanum d'Orb. station: — ? — ; habitat: Cuba; Brasils; d'Orb.!

T. antillarum d'Orb. (T. tuberosum Reeve station: on rocks in one to two feet water; Krebs! habitat: Antillae; Mörch! Cuba; Martinique; Guadeloupe; d'Orb.! Guadeloupe; Beau! St. Johns; Jamaica; Bermuda; C. B. Adams! St. Thomas; Tortola; Krebs!

T. aequale Reeve. station: — ? — ; habitat: Antillae; Mörch!

T. caribaeum d'Orb. station: — ? —; habitat: Pernambuco; Cuba; d'Orb.!

T. chlorostomum Lmk. station: — ? —; habitat:
Cuba; St. Lucy; Martinique; Guadeloupe; d'Orb.! Ja-
maica; St. Johns; Bermuda; C. B. Ad.! St. Thomas;
Krebs!

T. Cantrainii Recluz see Murex pauperculus Ad.

T. costatum Born. (T. succinctum Lmk.) station: — ?
—; habitat: Guadeloupe; Beau! Tortola; Krebs!

T. cynocephalum Lmk. station: — ? —; habitat:
Guadeloupe; Beau! St. Johns; Jamaica; Bermuda; C.
B. Adams! St. Croix; St. Martin; Trinidad; Krebs!

T. femorale L. station: on bluish, sandy mud together
with Strombus gallus Linne! habitat: Cuba; St. Lucy;
d'Orb.! Guadeloupe; Beau! St. Johns; Jamaica; C. B.
Adams! St. Thomas; St. Croix; St. Martin; Tortola;
Trinidad; Krebs!

T. labiosum Wood. (Tr. Loroisis Pt.) station: between
stones and coral-pieces on 2 feet water at St. Thomas;
Krebs! habitat: Antillae; Mörch! Guadeloupe; Duchassain! Beau! St. Thomas; St. Croix; St. Martin; Tortola; Krebs!

T. lanceolatum Mk. station: under stones and pieces
of corals in one and two feet water; Krebs! habitat:
Antillae; Mörch! Guadeloupe; Duchassain! Beau! St.
Thomas; St. Croix; Crabisland; Bermuda; Trinidad; St.
Martin; Anguilla; Krebs!

T. nobile Con. station: — ? —; habitat: Jamaica;
St. Johns; Cartagena! Nw.-Gr.; Bermuda; C. B. Ad.!

T. obscurum Reeve. station: — ? —; habitat: Jamaica; C. B. Adams! Guadeloupe; Beau! St. Croix;
Krebs!

T. martinianum d'Orb. station: — ? — ; habitat:
Cuba; Guadeloupe; St. Lucy; St. Thomas; d'Orb.! see
T. piliare Linné & Lmk.

T. parvum Ad. station: Between stones and pieces of
Madrepores on two feet water; Krebs! habitat: St.
Thomas; Anguilla; St. Barth; Krebs! St. Thomas; Ja-
maica; Rum-key, Turks-Island; C. B. Adams!

T. piliare L. & Lmk. (T. martinianum d'Orb.) Antillae;
Mörch! Guadeloupe; Beau! Jamaica; Carthagena in Nw.
Gr.; St. Johns; Bermuda; Sandwich Isl. C. B. Adams!
St. Thomas; Tortola; St. Martin; Barbadoes; Krebs!

T. pulchellum Ad. station: — ?; habitat: Jamaica;
C. B. Adams!

T. reticulare L. (T. clathratum Lmk.) Antillae; Mörch!
Guadeloupe; Duchassain! Beau! Jamaica; Carthagena in
Nw. Gren.; C. B. Adams! Tortola; Krebs!

T. rostratum Mart. (Fusus cutaceus L., Cassidaria cin-
gulata Lmk., Tr. undosum Kiener.) station: — ? ;
habitat: Antillae; Mörch!

T. testaceum Mörch. station: — ? — ; habitat: Antillae; Mörch! St. Thomas; St. Croix; St. Martin; Krebs!
remark: we have cause to believe that the localities
mentioned by C. B. Adams under the T. obscurus Reeve
are relative to Trit. testaceum. Mörch.

T. tigrinum Brod. station: — ? — ; habitat: Guadeloupe; Beau!

T. variegatum Lmk. (T. marmoratum Lmk.) station:
in two fathoms water on seaweed; habitat: Antillae;
Mörch! Guadeloupe; Duchassain! Beau! Vera-Cruz; St.
Thomas; Krebs!

T. vestitum Hinds. station: — ? ; habitat: Guadeloupe; Beau!

Ranella Lamarck.

R. crassa Desh. (R. granulata Lmk.) station: — ? ;
habitat: Guadeloupe; Beau! Hotessier!

R. cubaniana d'Orb. station: — ? —; habitat: Cuba;
St. Lucy; d'Orb.! Guadeloupe; Beau!

R. livida Reeve station: - ? ; habitat: Jamaica;
C. B. Adams!

R. rhodostoma: — ? ; station: — ? ; habitat: St.
Croix according to a label in the Academy of natural
sciences in Philadelphia; remark: the specimen in said
Academy appears very like R. Thomae d'Orb.

R. pondorosa Reeve. station: — ? ; habitat: Guadeloupe; Duchassain! Jamaica; C. B. Adams! Hamsbluff
at St. Croix; Krebs! remark: should Reeve's R. livida
not be young specimens of this shell? ; the figure and
the description in his Ic. conch. does not prove anything
to the contrary.

R. Thomae d'Orb. station: — ?; habitat: St. Thomas;
d'Orb.!

R. I sp. ind. We have further two specimens of Ranella
from St. Thomas, but we have not been able to find
any information about them.

Purpura Brugiére.

P. aberrans Ad. station: — ?; habitat: Jamaica; St.
Thomas; C. B. Adams!

P. bicostalis Lmk. station: on stones above low-water
mark; Krebs! habitat: Antillae; Mörch! Guadeloupe;
Beau; St. Thomas; Krebs!

P. fasciata Reeve. station: on stones above low-water
mark; Krebs! habitat: Gnadeloupe; Petit! Beau! St.

Johns; Jamaica; St. Thomas; C. B. Adams! St. Martha
and Carthagena in Nw. Gr.; Krebs!

P. **floridana** Con. station: Florida Reeve! Guadeloupe;
Petit! St. Thomas; Texas; Jamaica; C. B. Adams! Carthagena in Nw. Gr.; J. Redfield!

P. **galea** Chem. (P. abreviata Blv.) station: on perpendi-
cular rocks in 6 to 8 feet water; Krebs! habitat: Antillae; Mörch! Cuba; d'Orb.! Guadeloupe; Beau! St.
Thomas; St. Johns; Jamaica; C. B. Adams! St. Thomas!
St. Johns; Krebs!

P. **gibbosa** Reeve. station: — ? — ; habitat: Antillae; Mörch! St. Thomas; Krebs! Jamaica; C. B. Adams!
remark: Mörch thinks it may be a Rhizochilus of
Steenstrup.

P. **haemastoma** Lmk. station: — ? — ; habitat:
Guadeloupe; d'Orb.! St. Thomas; Krebs! remark: it
does not exactly live in the West-Indies, but is often
found at the bottom of vessels which arrive from the
coast of Africa at the port of St. Thomas.

P. **Kieneri** Desh. station: — ? ; habitat: Martinique
Lamarck! Philippines; Reeve! remark: we think the
last habitat to be correct as we never have seen a piece
of one between those thousand of West-Indian shells
which have passed through our hands.

P. **lineata** Lam. (B. bulbus Wood) station: — ? ; habitat: Antillae; Mörch!

P. **patula** Linné. station: on rocks at high water mark;
Krebs! habitat: Antillae; Mörch! Cuba; Martinique;
Guadeloupe; d'Orb.! St. Thomas; St. Martin; Carthagena
and St. Martha in New. Gr.; Krebs!

P. **plicata** Mart. station: on and in the roots of certain
species of Gorgonia in 2 to 3 fathoms water; Krebs!

habitat: Antillae; Mörch! St. Thomas; St. Johns; Anguilla; Krebs!

P. rustica Lam. station: — ? — ; habitat: Luzon (one of the Philippines) Reeve! Antillae; Mörch! St. Thomas; St. Martin; Krebs!

P. subdeltoidea Blainv. station: — ? — ; habitat: Cuba; Martinique; d'Orb.!

P. trapa Bolt. (P. deltoidea Lmk., M. nodus L., Meusch, Hippocastanum fasciatum Mart.) station: on rocks and stones at high-water mark; Krebs! habitat: Antillae; Mörch! Guadeloupe; Beau! Carthagena in Nw.-Gr.; Bermuda; Jamaica; C. B. Adams! St. Thomas; Krebs!

P. undata Lmk. station: — ? — ; habitat: Pernambuco; Cuba; d'Orb.! Guadeloupe; Beau!

P. vexillum Lmk. station: — ? —; habitat: Antilles; d'Orb.!

Recinula Lamarck.

R. ferruginosa Reeve. station: — ? —; habitat: Antillae; Mörch! remark: we think it is synonyme with R. nodulosa Ad.

R. nodulosa Ad. station: on stones in one to two feet water; Krebs! habitat: Guadeloupe; Beau! St. Thomas; St. Johns; St. Martha in New-Gr.; C. B. Adams! St. Thomas; St. Johns; St. Barth; St. Martin; Anguilla; Carthagena in New-Gr.; Krebs!

R. rosea Reeve. station: — ? — ; habitat: Island of Masbate; Reeve! St. Thomas; Krebs!

R. turbinella Kien. station: on stones in one to two feet water; Krebs! habitat: Guadeloupe; Beau! Duchassain! Petit! Jamaica; C. B. Adams! St. Thomas; St. Barth; Anguilla; St. Martin; Krebs!

Columbella Lamarck.

C. argus d'Orb. station: — ? — ; habitat: Guadeloupe; Hotessier! Beau!

C. atomella Ducl. station: — ? — ; habitat: West-Indies; Guilding! according to a note of C. B. Adams!

C. barbadensis d'Orb. station: — ? — ; habitat: Antilles; d'Orb.!

C. Broderipii Sow. station: — ? —; habitat: Guadeloupe; Beau!

C. catenata Sowb. (Buccinum mitrula Dk.) station: under pieces of Madrepores on 1 à 2 feet water Krebs! habitat: Guadeloupe: Beau! Jamaica; C. B. Adams! St. Thomas; St. Johns; St. Martin; Krebs!

C. corniculata Ad. station: — ?; habitat: Jamaica; C. B. Adams!

C. decipiens Ad. (Bucc. concinnum Ad.) station: — ? — ; habitat: Jamaica; C. B. Adams! St. Thomas; Krebs! remark: perhaps synonyme with C. subcostata Ad.

C. dermestoides Kiener. station: — ? — ; habitat: West-Indies; Sowerby! Guadeloupe; Beau!

C. dichroa Sowb. station: — ? — ; habitat: St. Vincent; Guilding! Jamaica; C. B. Adams!

C. dormitor Sowb. (Col. purpurascens Ad.) station: — ? — : habitat: St. Vincent; Guilding! Jamaica; C. B. Ad.!

C. Ducloziana d'Orb. station: — ? — ; habitat: St. Thomas; Jamaica; d'Orb.!

C. fastigata Kien. station: — ? — ; habitat: les iles saintes Kien. according to C. B. Adams!

C. fenestrata Ad. station: — ? — ; habitat: Jamaica! C. B. Adams! St. Thomas; Krebs!

C. fusiformis d'Orb. station: — ? — ; habitat: Martinique; Jamaica; d'Orb.!

C. Guildingii Sowb. station: — ? — ; habitat: St. Vincent; Guilding!

C. Hotessieri d'Orb.! station: — ? — ; habitat: Guadeloupe; Hotessier! Beau!

C. lactea Sowb. station: — ? — ; habitat: Antillae; Mörch!

C. laevigata Lmk. (Col. concinna Sowb.) station: — ? — ; Antillae; Mörch! Jamaica; St. Johns; Arecibo; C. B. Adams! Guadeloupe; Beau! Duchassain! Carthagena in New-Gr.; Redfield! St. Thomas; St. Croix; St. Martin; Trinidad; St. Martha in New-Gr.; Krebs!

C. la Fresnayi. Fisch & Bern. station: — ? — ; habitat: Marie Galante; Beau!

C. mercatoria L. station: between sea-weed on sandy ground on 2 to 4 feet water; habitat: Cuba; Martinique; Guadeloupe; St. Lucy; Jamaica; d'Orb.! St. Johns; Jamaica; Bermuda; Turksisland; Arecibo; C. B. Adams! St. Thomas; St. Croix; St. Barth; St. Martin; Anguilla; Barbadoes; Trinidad; Carthagena in New-Gr.; Krebs!

C. nitida Lmk. (S. nitidula (L.?) Sowb.) station: under pieces of corals on 2 to 3 feet water; habitat: Guadeloupe; Martinique; St. Lucy; Cuba; d'Orb.! St. Johns! Arecibo; C. B. Adams! St. Thomas; St. Johns; St. Croix; St. Barth; Anguilla; St. Martin; Barbadoes; Krebs! remark: d'Orbigny makes the remark that this species deminishes in size from Guadeloupe toward Cuba; we have seen very large specimens said to come from Margarita.

C. obesa Ad. station: — ? — ; habitat: Jamaica; C. B. Adams! Guadeloupe; Beau! St. Thomas; Carthagena; New-Gr.; Krebs!

C. monolifera Sowb. station: — ? — ; habitat: West-Indies; Jay's Catalogue!

C. ocellata d'Orb. (pt. 2 pg. 135) station: — ? — ; habitat: Cuba; St. Lucy; d'Orb.!

C. ocellata Gml. station: under stones on 1 to 2 feet water; Krebs! habitat: Jamaica; Bermuda; C. B. Adams! Guadeloupe; Beau! Duchassain! St. Thomas; St. Johns; St. Croix; St. Barth; Anguilla; St. Martin; Krebs! remark: in a manuscript of C. B. Adams stands C. parvula Dunker (Philippi?) and C. guttata Sowb. as synonymes of this species, but the firts mentioned species is surely destinct.

C. ovulata Lmk. station: under pieces of madrepores on stony ground in 1 to 2 feet water; Krebs! habitat: Cuba; Guadeloupe; St. Lucy; d'Orb.! Jamaica; C. B. Adams! St. Thomas; St. Croix; St. Barth; Anguilla; St. Martin; Krebs!

C. ovuloides Ad. station: — ? — ; habitat: Turks Island; C. B. Adams! remark: surely synonyme with C. ovulata. Lmk.

G. Peleci Kiener. (C. rudis Sowb.) station: — ? — ; habitat: Martinique; Kiener! Nevis; Sowerby!

C. parvula Ph. station: — ? — ; habitat: St. Thomas; St. Johns; St. Martin; Krebs!

C. pulchella Kiener (Buc. triticum Sol.) habitat: Guadeloupe; Beau! St. Thomas; St. Johns; St. Croix; St. Martin; Anguilla; Krebs!

C. pusilla Sowb. station: — ? — ; habitat: St. Vincent; Guilding! Jamaica; C. B. Adams!

C. rudis Sowb. (C. Peleci Kien.).

C. Sagra d'Orb.! station: — ? — ; habitat: Guadeloupe; d'Orb.! Beau!

C. Schrammii Petit. station: — ? —; habitat: Guadeloupe; Beau!

C. subcostata Ad. station: under pieces of madrepores
on 1 foot water; Krebs! habitat: Guadeloupe; Beau!
Duchassain! Petit! Jamaica; Turks-Island; Bahama; C.
B. Adams! St. Thomas! St. Johns; St. Croix; St. Barth;
St. Martin; Anguilla; Trinidad; Krebs!

C. therpsichore Leathes. station: — ? —; habitat:
Antillae; Mörch! Nevis; Cuming! West-Indies; Lmk.!
South sea; Kiener!

Pisania Bivona.

P. pennata Brown. (B. plumatum Gm.; Fusus articulatus
Lmk.; Murex accinctus Born; Purpura accincta d'Orb.)
station: — ? — ; habitat: Cuba; St. Lucy; Guadeloupe; Jamaica; d'Orb.! Honduras; Reeve! St. Johns! E.
Hartwig! Tortola?; Krebs! remark: it is rare, if at all
found at the Virgin Islands.

P. tritones Reeve station: — ? —; habitat: Antillae;
Mörch!

Nassa Lamarck.

N. albescens Dunk. station: — ? —; habitat: West-
Indies; Reeve!

N. antillarum d'Orb. station: — ? —; habitat: Guadeloupe; Beau!

N. (Phos) antillarum Phil. (B. zonale Brug) station:
Antillae; Mörch! Cuba; Reeve! Guadeloupe; Beau! St.
Thomas and Carthagena in New-Gr.; Krebs!

N. ambigua Pult. station: — ? — ; habitat: Guadeloupe; Beau! Jamaica; Turks-Island; C. B. Adams! St.
Thomas; St. Croix; St. Barth; Anguilla; Krebs!

N. (Phos) Beauii Fisch. & Bern. station: — ? —; habitat: Marie Galante; Beau!

N. Candei d'Orb. station: — ? —; Guadeloupe; Beau! de Cande!

N. candidissima Ad. station: — ? —; habitat: Jamaica; C. B. Adams!

N. (Phos) guadeloupensis Petit. station: Between stones on 1 foot water at Carthagena; Krebs! habitat: Guadeloupe; Petit! Beau! St. Johns; Cartagena in New-Granada; C. B. Adams! St. Thomas; St. Martha in New-Gran.; Krebs!

N. Hotessieri d'Orb. station: — ? —; habitat: Jamaica; Guadeloupe; Martinique; d'Orb.! (Moll. de Cuba pt. 2 pg. 142 pl. 21 fig. 40, 42).

N. olivacea Desh. station: — ? —; habitat: West-Indies; Jay's Catalogue! Reeve! Guadeloupe; Lamarck!

N. polygona Lmk. station: — ? —; habitat: Cuba; Martinique; Guadeloupe; Rio-Janeiro; d'Orb.! Moll. de Cuba pt. 2 140.

N. (Strongylocera) textilina Mörch. station: — ? —; habitat: Antillae; Mörch!

N. vibex Say. station: — ? —; habitat: Guadeloupe; Beau!

Buccinum Linné.

B. auriculatum Lmk. (B. coromandelinum Lmk., B. Caribaeorum d'Orb.) station: between large rocks and in excavations of rocks & madrepores near the shore; habitat: Jamaica; St. Martha; Carthagena; C. B. Adams! St. Thomas; St. Croix: St. Martha; Krebs! remark: on a lable of C. B. Adams stands: „B. corom. Lmk. (Pollia tincta Conr. ?)“

B. pulchellum Ad. station: — ? — ; habitat: Jamaica; St. Thomas; C. B. Adams!

Bullia Gray.

B. aciculata Lmk. (Bucc. monile Linné? Mörch) station:
— ? — ; habitat: Antillae?; Mörch! Guadeloupe;
Beau! Duchassain!

B. — ? station: — ? — ; habitat: St. Barth and Anguilla; Krebs!

Terebra Adanson.

T. castanea Kien. station: — ? —; habitat: Guadeloupe; Beau!

T. cinerea Born. station: — ? — ; habitat: Antillae;
(T. accicularis Lmk.) Mörch! Guadeloupe; St. Lucy; Cuba;
d'Orb. !

T. hastata Gml. (syn: T. lancinula Gml. acc. to Mörch;
T. costata acc. to C. B. Adams) station: — ? — ; ha-
bitat: Antillae; Mörch! St. Johns; Jamaica; C. B.
Adams! Guadeloupe; Beau! Anguilla; Krebs!

T. jamaicensis Ad. station: it buries itself in white
sand at low-water mark; habitat: St. Johns; Jamaica;
Arecibo; C. B. Adams! Guadeloupe; Beau! St. Thomas;
Krebs!

T. rudis Gray. station: — ? — ; habitat: St. Lucy;
d'Orb. !

T. sp. ind. station: — ? — ; habitat: St. Martha,
New-Gr. in the collection of H. Krebs!

Cancellaria Lamarck.

C. Candei d'Orb. station: — ? — ; habitat: Martinique; de Cande!

C. reticulata L. station: — ? — ; habitat: Cuba; Guadeloupe; d'Orb.! Marie-Galante; Beau! St. Thomas; Tortola; St. Martin; Krebs!

C. rugosa Lmk. station: — ? — ; habitat: Guadeloupe; St. Thomas; Tortola; C. B. Adams! St. Thomas; Anguilla; St. Martin; Krebs! Marie-Galante; Beau!

Cassis Lamarck.

1. Semicassis Kleiner.

C. abbreviata Lmk. (C. lactea Kiener) station: — ? — ; habitat: Antillae; Mörch! Guadeloupe; Beau! St. Thomas; Krebs!

C. bisulcata Wag? station: — ? — ; habitat: Antillae; Mörch!

C. cicatricosa Meusch. (C. recurvirostris Gml. non Reeve; C. granulosa jun. Kien.) station: Antillae; Mörch! Guadeloupe; Beau! Duchassain! St. Thomas; St. Johns; Jamaica; Carthagena; North-Caroline; C. B. Adams! Tortola; St. Croix; Krebs!

C. cornuta L. (C. labiata Chem.) station: — ? — ; habitat: Guadeloupe; Beau!

C. gibba Gml. (C. globulus Bolt.; C. abreviata Lmk.; acc. to Mörch!) station: Antillae;. Mörch! Carthagena; St. Martin; Krebs!

C. ventricosa Mart. (Cass. granulosa Lmk.; B. granulatum Born according to Mörch! Bucc. tessellatum Chem. according to Beau!) station: at certain seasons of the year in seaweed on 2 to 3 feet water and on the white sand on the beach; Krebs! habitat: Antillae; Mörch! Guadeloupe; Beau! St. Thomas; Krebs!

2. Cassis Browne.

C. flammea L. station: in 3 fathoms water on seaweed;

Krebs! habitat: Antillae; Mörch! Cuba; d'Orb.! Jamaica; C. B. Adams! Guadeloupe; Beau! Barbadoes; Antigua; Tortola; Krebs!

C. **Madegascariensis** Lmk. station: — ? — ; habitat: Antillae; Mörch! Jamaica; C. B. Adams! St. Thomas; St. Croix; Krebs!

C. **tuberosa** L. station: — ? — ; habitat: Antillae; Mörch! Cuba; d'Orb.! Jamaica; Bermuda; C. B. Adams! Guadeloupe; Beau! Duchassain! Antigua; St. Johns; Tortola; St. Martin; Barbadoes; Krebs!

3. Cypræcassis Stutschb.

C. **testiculus** L. (C. crumena Brug. accord. to C. B. Ad.!) station: — ? — ; habitat: St. Johns; Jamaica; Arecibo; Carthagena; Bermuda; C. B. Adams! Guadeloupe; Beau! St. Croix; Tortola; St. Barth; Barbadoes; Trinidad; Carthagena; Krebs!

Oniscia Lamarck.

O. **Denisonii** Reeve. station: — ? — ; habitat: Guadeloupe; Beau!

O. **Oniscus** L. station: — ? — ; habitat: Guadeloupe; Beau! St. Johns; St. Thomas; Jamaica; Arecibo; C. B. Adams! St. Thomas; Tortola; St. Barth; Anguilla; St. Martin; Trinidad; Krebs!

Dolium Lamarck.

D. **galea** L.? station: — ? — ; habitat: St. Thomas; R. Swift! Jamaica; C. B. Adams!

D. **pennatum** Mart. station: — ? — ; habitat: St. Johns; Jamaica; C. B. Adams! Guadeloupe; Beau! St. Johns; Tortola; St. Martin; St. Barth; Barbadoes; Trinidad; Krebs! remark: C. B. Adams above mentioned habitats are marked by D. perdix L. which is an East-India shell.

Eburnea Lamarck.

E. **balteata** Sow. station: — ? —; habitat: Antillae; Mörch!

E. **glabrata** Lmk. station: — ? —; habitat: Curaçao; R. Swift! Jamaica; Curaçao; de Candé!

E. **Tankervillii** Swains. station: — ? —; Jsland of Margarita; Swift!

Volutacea.
Voluta Linné.

V. **Beauii** Fischer & Bern. station: — ? —; habitat: Marie Galante; Beau!

V. **musica** L. station: — ? —; habitat: Cuba; Guadeloupe; St. Lucy; d'Orb.! Guadeloupe; Beau! Margarita; R. Swift! Barbadoes; Krebs! remark: not heatherto found at the Virgin-Islands; the largest ever seen were from the island of Margarita.

V. **Guildingii** Sowb. station: — ? —; habitat: St. Vincent; Reeve! remark: Reeve's drawing of this shell the Ic. conch. looks very much like Mitra dermestina Lamarck.

V. **Vespertilio** Rumphius. station: — ? —; habitat: Antilles; d'Orb.!

Mitra Lamarck.

M. **alreolata** Reeve. station: — ? —; habitat: Antillae; Mörch!

M. **barbadensis** Gmelin. (M. striatula Lmk.) station: on coral-reefs according to Guilding! habitat: St. Vincent;

Reeve! Cuba; de la Sagra! Auber! Martinique; Candé!
Guadeloupe; Beau! Duchassain! Hotessier! St. Thomas;
St. Johns; St. Barth; St. Martin; Barbadoes; Krebs!

M. candida Reeve. station: — ? — ; habitat: St.
Thomas; Lillienskjold! Mörch! Krebs! St. Croix;
Krebs! remark: It is pale yellow or pink when very
fresh and perfect.

M. caelagaena Reeve. station: — ? — ; habitat:
Crabisland; A. H. Riise! St. Thomas; Krebs!

M. cavea Reeve. station: — ? — ; habitat: Guadeloupe; Beau! remark: see M. microzonias var. bifasciata.

M. dermestina Lmk. (M. speciosa Reeve? Mörch!) station: — ? — ; habitat: Antillae; Mörch! St. Thomas;
St. Johns; Passage-Island; St. Martin; Anguilla; Krebs!

M. microzonias Reeve? station: — ? — ; habitat:
Antillae; Mörch!

M. microzonias var. bifasciata (M. cavea Reeve; M.
microzonias Kiener.)

M. nodulosa Gml. (M. granulosa Lmk.) station: on rocks
Guilding! habitat: St. Vincent; Reeve! Cuba; de la
Sagra! Auber! St. Lucy; Martinique; Guadeloupe; Candé!
Hotessier! St. Thomas; St. Johns; Krebs!

M. nucleola Reeve. Does the drawing in Reeve's Ic. conch.
not represent a M. nodulosa Gml.?

M. pulchella Reeve. station: — ? — ; habitat: Barbadoes; Humphreys! Guadeloupe; Beau! remark: is it
not synonyme with M. derme. Lmk.?

M. semicostata Anton. station: — ? — ; habitat: St.
Croix; St. Martin; Anguilla; Krebs!

M. sulcata Gml. (M. microzonias Lmk.) station: — ? — ;
habitat: Antillae; Mörch!

M. sulcata bifasciata (M. cavea R.! M. microz. K.)

M. puella Reeve. station: — ? —; habitat: St. Thomas; Gruner! Guadeloupe; Beau! St. Thomas; St. Croix; St. Johns; St. Martin; Krebs!

M. tiarella Lmk. station: — ? — ; habitat: West-Indies; Jay's Catalogue!

Oliva Brugiére.

O. angulata Lmk. (V. incrassata Sol., V. corticata & striatula Mart.) station: — ? — ; habitat: Antillae; Mörch!

O. atennata Reeve. station: — ? — ; habitat: Cuba; C. B. Adams!

O. bullula Reeve. station: — ? —; habitat: Guadeloupe; Beau! St. Thomas; St. Barth; Krebs!

O. dealbata Reeve. station: — ? —; habitat: Guadeloupe; Beau!

O. Esther Ducl. station: — ? — ; habitat: Antillae, Mörch!

O. exigua Mart. (O. conoidalis Lmk.; Voluta jaspidea Gml.; Olivina d'Orb.) station: — ? — ; habitat: Curaçao; Candé! Cuba; de la Sagra! Guadeloupe; Hotessier! St. Johns; Jamaica; Carthagena; Tortola; C. B. Adams! Barbadoes; Curaçao; St. Thomas; Krebs!

O. flammulata Lmk. (Mica marmorata Mart.) station: — ? —; habitat: Antillae; Mörch!

O. fimbriata Reeve. station: — ? —; habitat: Guadeloupe; Beau! St. Johns; Barbadoes; Jamaica; South-Caroline; Brasils; Maracaibo; Carthagena; C. B. Adams!

O. fulgida Reeve. station: — ? —; habitat: St. Thomas; St. Barth; Anguilla; Krebs! Guadeloupe; Beau!

O. Guildingii Reeve. station: — ? —; habitat: St. Vincent; Reeve! Jamaica; C. B. Adams!

O. ispida Link. (O. fusiformis Link.) station: — ?
— ; habitat: Guadeloupe; Beau! Jamaica; C. B.
Adams! Great North-Side-Bay at St. Thomas; Krebs!

O. leucostoma Ducl. (O. ancillaria d'Orb.) station: — ?
— ; habitat: Antillae; d'Orb.!

O. ligneola Reeve. station: — ? — ; habitat: Gua-
ranao in Venezuela; Swift!

O. litterata Lmk. station: — ? — ; habitat: Antillae;
Mörch! Florida; R. Swift! Bermuda; C. B. Adams!
Vera-Cruz; Krebs!

O. mica Ducl. station: — ? — ; habitat: Jamaica; de
Candé!

O. miliola d'Orb. station: — ? — ; habitat: Jamaica;
Martinique; de Candé!

O. millepunctata Ducl. station: — ? — ; West-Indies;
Reeve! Antillae; Mörch!

O. minuta Link. (O. ziczac Ducl.) station: — ? — ;
habitat: Antillae; Mörch!

O. mitrola Ducl. station: — ? — ; habitat: Antillae;
Mörch!

O. myriadina Ducl. station: — ? — ; habitat: Cuba;
de la Sagra! St. Thomas & Jamaica; de Candé! Jamaica;
Bahamas; C. B. Adams!

O. nana Lmk. (O. micans Sol.) station: — ? — ; habitat: West-Indies; Reeve! Jamaica; de Candé! Antillae;
Mörch! remark: should this not be synonyme with O.
strigata Reeve?

O. nitidula Link. (O. mutica R.) station: — ? — ; habitat: Guadeloupe; Beau! South - Caroline; Jamaica;
Portocabello; C. B. Adams! St. Thomas; St. Barth; Bahama; Krebs!

O. nivea d'Orb. station: — ? — ; habitat: St. Barth

de Candé! Guadeloupe; Hotessier! Cuba; de la Sagra! Auber! Florida; d'Orb.!

O. oryza Lmk. station: — ? —; habitat: Guadeloupe; Beau! Bermuda; Bahama; Jamaica; C. B. Adams! St. Barth; St. Martin; Krebs!

O. parvula Mart. (Voluta nivea Ginl., Olivina d'Orb., Oliva eburnea Lmk.) station: —-? —; habitat: St. Barth; de Candé; Guadeloupe; Hotessier! Beau! Cuba; de la Sagra! Auber! Florida; d'Orbig.! Jamaica; C. B. Adams! St. Thomas; St. Croix; St. Barth; Anguilla; Barbadoes; Krebs! remark: we have specimens with gray, yellow, orange and rose ornaments; is it not synonyme with Oliva nana Lmk.?

O. pulchella Duclos. station: — ? —; habitat: Florida; Jamaica; C. B. Adams! St. Thomas; Krebs! remark: very closely allied with O. lanceolata R.; we have seen specimens of O. pulch. Duc. with spots close to the suture.

O. pura Reeve. station: — ? —; habitat: St. Martin?; Krebs!

O. reticularis Lmk. (O. olivaceus Mensch) station: we suppose it buries itself in sand; a very young life specimen has been dredged from blue sandy mud in 10 to 12 fathoms water; habitat: Cuba; Auber! St. Lucy; Guadeloupe; Hotessier! Florida; Alphen! Jamaica; Carthagena; Curaçao: Cumana; Bermuda; C. B. Adams! Guadeloupe; Beau! St. Thomas; St. Johns; St. Croix; St. Barth; Tortola; St. Martin; Anguilla; Trinidad; Sta. Martha in New-Granada; Krebs! remark: Bean gives as synonymes O. arancosa Lmk., O. timoria Ducl., O. venulata Ducl., O. obesina Ducl., O. pindarina Ducl.

O. **rosalina** Duclos. station: — ? — ; habitat: Guadeloupe; Duchassain! Jamaica; Turks-Island; C. B. Adams!

O. **rufifasciata** Reeve. station: — ? — ; habitat: St. Thomas; Krebs! remark: nothing else than a variety of O. nitidula Link.

O. **scripta** Lmk. station: — ? — ; habitat: Guadeloupe; Beau! Jamaica; C. B. Adams! Curaçao; St. Lucy; Cuba; d'Orbigny!

O. **strigata** Reeve. station: — ? —; habitat: Hatfield, Jamaica; E. Chitty!

Cypraeaceae.

Cypraea Linné.

C. **bicallosa** Gray. station: — ? — ; habitat: Marie Galante; Beau!

C. **cervus** L. (C. cervina Lmk.) station: — ? — ; habitat: Antillae; Mörch!

C. **cornea** Gray (C. rosea Kien.) station: — ? —; habitat: Guadeloupe; Beau!

C. **exanthema** L. station: — ? — ; habitat: Cuba; de la Sagra! Auber! Martinique; Guadeloupe; St. Lucy! de Candé! Hotessier! Duchassain! Beau! St. Thomas; St. Barth; St. Martin; Krebs!

C. **globosa** Sow. (C. pilula Kiener.) station: — ? — ; habitat: Cuba; Auber! New-Orleans; d'Orbigny! Guadeloupe; Beau! St. Thomas; St. Croix; St. Johns; St. Barth; Anguilla; Krebs!

C. **mus** L. station: — ? — : habitat; Cuba; de la Sagra! Martinique; de Candé! Curaçao; R. Swift!

C. **nivea** Gray. station: — ? —; habitat: Guadeloupe; Beau! Cuba; Auber! New-Orleans; d'Orbigny!

C. **pediculus** L. station: — ? —; habitat: Cuba; de

la Sagra! Martinique; de Candé! Guadeloupe; Hotessier! Beau! St. Thomas; St. Croix; St. Johns; Tortola; St. Martin; St. Barth; Anguilla; Barbadoes; Trinidad; Krebs!

C. rotunda Kiener (C. qvadripunctata Gray) station: — ? — ; habitat: Cuba; St. Lucy; New-Orleans; d'Orb.! St. Thomas; St. Croix; St. Johns; St. Barth; St. Martin; Anguilla; Barbadoes; Trinidad; Jamaica; Krebs!

C. spurca Linné (C. flaveola Reeve; C. iota Born) station: — ? — ; habitat: Martinique; St. Lucy; Cuba; d'Orbigny! Guadeloupe; Beau! St. Thomas; St. Croix; St. Martin; Barbadoes; Krebs!

C. stercoraria L. station: — ? — ; habitat: Guadeloupe; Beau!

C. succincta L. (C. cinerea Mart.; C. sordida Lmk.) station: — ? — ; habitat: St. Thomas; Tortola; St. Barth; St. Martin; Anguilla; Barbadoes; St. Domingo; Krebs! Cuba; Martinique; Jamaica; d'Orbigny! Guadeloupe; Beau! Duchassain!

C. suffusa Gray (C. armindina Ducl.) station: — ? — ; habitat: Guadeloupe; Beau! St. Thomas; St. Croix; St. Barth; St. Martin; Anguilla; Barbadoes; Krebs!

C. subrostrata Gray. station: — ? — ; habitat: Guadeloupe; Beau! St. Thomas; St. Johns; St. Croix; St. Barth; Anguilla; Barbadoes; Krebs! remark: we have beside a white variety.

C. tremeza Ducl. station: — ? — ; habitat: West-Indies; Reeve!

Erato Risso.

E. Maugeriae Gray. station: dredged from blue sandy mud in 10 to 12 fathoms water; habitat: St. Thomas; St. Barth; Krebs! Guadeloupe; Beau!

Ovula Brugiére.

O. acicularis Lmk. station: — ? — ; habitat: Cuba; d'Orbigny! St. Martin; Krebs! Guadeloupe; Beau!

O. gibbosa Lmk. station: — ? — ; habitat: Cuba; de la Sagra! Auber! Martinique; Guadeloupe; St. Lucy; Hotessier! de Candé! Guadeloupe; Beau! St. Thomas; St. Johns; Anguilla; Trinidad; Krebs!

Marginella Lamarck.

M. albolineata d'Orb. station: — ? — ; habitat: Cuba; Auber! Jamaica; C. B. Adams!

M. apicina Mke. (M. flavida Redf.) station: — ? — ; habitat: Bahama; Redfield! St. Thomas; Swift! Krebs!

M. avena Kien. station: — ? — ; habitat: Cuba; Auber! de Candé!

M. candida Redf. station: — ? — ; habitat: St. Thomas; St. Croix; St. Barth; Anguilla; Krebs!

M. caribaea d'Orb. station: — ? — ; habitat: Cuba; de la Sagra! Auber! St. Thomas; de Candé! remark: described in d'Orbigny's Moll. de Cuba pt. 2 pg. 97.

M. catenata Mont. station: — ? — ; habitat: Spanishtown; St. Martin; St. Barth; Guadeloupe; Krebs!

M. chrysomelina Redf. station: — ? — ; habitat: West-Indies; Krebs!

M. conoidalis Kiener. station: — ? — ; habitat: Antillae; Mörch! Havana; Jay! remark: is this not synonyme with M. apicina Mencke?

M. crassilabrum Sowb. station: — ? — ; habitat: West-Indies; Jay!

M. Delessertiana Recluz. station: — ? — ; habitat: Guadeloupe; Beau!

M. interrupta-lineata Muhlf. (M. interrupta Lmk.) sta-

tion: — ? — ; habitat: Antillae; Mörch! Carthagena;
St. Martha; Redfield! St. Thomas; d'Orbigny! St. Martha; Carthagena in New - Granada; Krebs! remark:
d'Orbigny's locality „St. Thomas" is surely a mistake;
he may have bought it or received it from a collector
in said place, but we doubt that it has been found at
the island of St. Thomas, where we have collected shells
in 17 years and never seen a trace of it; Mr. J. Redfield
has told us that he always received M. interrupta-lineata
Muhlf. and M. obesa Redf. intermixed when the shells
came from Carthagena, but only M. interrupta-l. when
they came from Sta. Martha; Mr. Cotoy has told R.
Swift Esq. that he M. int-st. was always found along
the shore and M. ob. in 8 to 10 fathoms of water.

M. frumentum Sowb. station: — ? — ; habitat:
West-Indies; Jay!

M. fusca Sowb. station: — ? — ; habitat: West-Indies; Jay!

M. glans Mencke. station: — ? — ; habitat: St. Domingo; Jay!

M. lactea Kiener (Pers. parva Mart.) station: — ? — ;
habitat: Antillae; Mörch! Guadeloupe; Beau!

M. Lavelleana d'Orb. (M. minima Guild.) station: — ?
— ; habitat: Jamaica; Martinique; de Candé! St. Thomas; R. Swift! Krebs!

M. longivaricosa Lmk. station: — ? — ; habitat:
Cuba; Sagra!

M. maculosa Kien. station: — ? — ; habitat: Curaçao;
R. Swift!

M. marginata Born. (M. bivaricosa Lmk.) station: — ?
— ; habitat: Antilläe; de Candé! Mörch! Curaçao; R.
Swift! Sta. Martha; Krebs!

M. muralis Hinds. station: — ? — ; habitat: Curaçao; Mörch! Jamaica; Jay!

M. nivea Ad. station: — ? — ; habitat: Jamaica; Jay!

M. obesa Redfield (M. similis Sowb.) station: in 8 to 10 fathoms water along the coast of Venezuela and New-Granada; habitat: Sta. Martha; Redfield! Cartha-gena; Jay!

M. ovuliformis d'Orb. station: — ? — ; habitat: Martinique; Guadeloupe; St. Thomas; de Candé! Gua-deloupe; Beau!

M. pallida L. (M. avenacea Desh.) station: — ? — ; habitat: St. Thomas; St. Johns; St. Martin; St. Barth; Barbadoes; Krebs! Honduras; Jay! St. Domingo; Gua-deloupe; de Candé! Cuba; Auber! Guadeloupe; Beau! remark: (Beau has as synonymes: M. avena. Kien. & M. varia. Sow. *Entirlij di fleion* ʔ ʔ

M. pellucida Pfr. (M. diaphana Ki.) station: — ? — ; habitat: Antillae; Mörch! St. Thomas; R. Swift! Krebs!

M. phrygia Sowb. station: — ? — ; habitat: Antil-lae; Mörch!

M. pulcherrima Ad. station: — ? — ; habitat: Ba-hama; Redf! remark: very like M. catenata Mont., but only ornamented with white spots, not with lines.

M. pulchra Gray. station: — ? — ; habitat: St. Domingo; Jay!

M. rubella Ad. station: — ? — ; habitat: Jamaica; Adams! Jay! St. Thomas; Krebs!

M. subcoerulea Mart. (V. prunum. Gm., V. coerulescens Lmk.) station: Antillae; Mörch! Curaçao; Candé! Swift! Guadeloupe; Beau! Sta. Martha; Krebs!

M. sulcata d'Orb. station: in mud on 4 to 6 fathoms

water; habitat: Martinique; Candé! St. Thomas; A. H. Riise!

M. subtriplicata d'Orb. station: — ? — ; habitat: St. Barth; St. Thomas; Candé! Guadeloupe; Beau! Guadeloupe; St. Martin; Anguilla; St. Johns; Krebs!

M. tesselata Lmk. station: — ? — ; habitat: Venezuela; Jay!

M. zonata Kien. station: — ? — ; habitat: West-Indies; Jay!

M. xanhostoma Mörch station: — ? — ; habitat: Curaçao; Mörch!

Volvaria Lamarck.

V. pellucida Schm. (V. pallida Lmk. non L.) station: — ? — ; habitat: Guadeloupe; d'Orb.! Beau! Duchassin! St. Thomas; St. Johns; St. Barth; Anguilla; St. Martin; Barbadoes; Krebs!

Turritella Lamarck.

T. bicingulata Lmk. (Xylohelix T. marmorcus minor Chem.) station: — ? — ; habitat: Antillac; Mörch!

T. caribaea d'Orb. station: — ? — ; habitat: Cuba; Sagra!

T. exoleta L. (Haustator Mtf.; Terebellum Browne; T. torcularis Born according to Beau) station: — ? — ; habitat: Jamaica; C. B. Adams! Guadeloupe; Beau! Porto-Plata; St. Martin; Trinidad; Krebs!

T. imbricata L. station: — ? — ; habitat: Antillac; Lamarck! Mörch! Jamaica; St. Lucy; d'Orbigny!

T. Meta Reeve. station: — ? — ; habitat: St. Martha; Carthagena; Krebs! remark: perhaps a variety of T. imbr. L.

T. variegata (T. marmoratus Ch.; Elob. marmoreum Bolt.,
T. imbricata Lmk.) station: — ? — ; habitat: An-
tillae; Mörch! Jamaica; St. Lucy; d'Orbigny! Carthagena;
Redfield! Cumana; J. H. Newton! Island of Margarita
and at Mayaguez in Puertorico; R. Swift! St. Thomas;
Krebs!

Cerithium Adanson.

C. albovittatum Ad. station: — ? — ; habitat: Jamaica; C. B. Adams! remark: described in „Contributions" No 7 page 122.

C. algicola Ad. station: — ? — ; habitat: Rum-Key,
Turks-Island; Bahama; Jamaica; C. B. Adams! St. Thomas; Porto-Plata; Barbadoes; Krebs!

C. ambiguum Ad. (synonymes according to Beau: C. costatum Wood, C. servile C. B. Ad.) station: — ? —;
habitat: Jamaica; C. B. Adams! Guadeloupe; Beau!
remark: described in „Proceedings of the Boston Soc.
of Nat. History". Jan. 1st. 1845 page 4.

C. atratum Born. station: on rocks close to the shore
between the marks of high and low water; at other
seasons on blue sandy mud in 2 fathoms water; habitat: Guadeloupe; Lamarck! Beau! Rio-Janeiro; Jamaica;
C. B. Adams! Key West; J. H. Newton! St. Thomas;
Krebs!

C. bicolor Ad. station: — ? — ; habitat: Jamaica;
C. B. Adams! St. Thomas; Th. Bland! Arecibo; J. H.
Newton! remark: described in the „Proceedings of the
Boston. S. of Nat. Sc." 1st January 1845 page 5.

C. columellare d'Orb. station: — ? — ; habitat:
St. Thomas; Guadeloupe; St. Domingo; Jamaica; Cuba;
Candé! Guadeloupe; Beau!

C. **dissimile** Yoldi station: — ? — ; habitat: Antillae; Mörch!

C. **eburneum** Brug. station: — ? — ; habitat: Antilles; Lamarck! Guadeloupe; Martinique; Cuba; d'Orb.! Guadeloupe; Beau! St. Thomas; Krebs!

C. **eriense** Kien. station: — ? — ; habitat: Guadeloupe; Beau!

C. **exile** Ad. station: — ? — ; habitat: Jamaica; C. B. Adams! remark: described in „Contributions" No 7 April 1850 page 120.

C. **ferrugineum** Say. station: — ? — ; habitat: Guadeloupe; Beau!

C. **flavum** Ad. station: — ? — ; habitat: Jamaica; C. B. Adams! remark: described in „Contributions" No 7 page 122 April 1850.

C. **fusiforme** Ad. station: — ? — ; habitat: Jamaica; C. B. Adams! remark: described in „Contributions" No 7 page 120 April 1850.

C. **gemmulosum** Ad. station: — ? —; habitat: Jamaica; C. B. Adams! St. Thomas; Krebs! remark: described in „Contributions" No 7 page 120 April 1850.

C. **gibberulum** Ad. station: in myriades on mud in 8 to 15 fathoms water; habitat: Jamaica; C. B. Adams! St. Thomas; St. Johns; St. Martin; Porto-Plata; Krebs! remark: described in the „Proc. of the Boston S. of Nat. History" 1st January 1845 page 5.

C. **interruptum** Mke.? station: — ? — ; habitat: Saba; R. Swift! St. Thomas; St. Martin; Porto-Plata; Krebs!

C. **iota** Ad. station: — ? —; habitat: Jamaica; Ad.! remark: described in „Proc. of the Boston S. of Nat. History" January 1st 1845.

C. Lafondii Mich. station: — ? —; habitat: Mediter-
ranian sea; Lmk.! Jamaica; Ad.!

C. Lavalleanum d'Orb. station: — ? — ; habitat:
Cuba; d'Orb.!

C. lima Brug. station: — ? —; habitat: Guadeloupe;
Lmk.! d'Orb.! Beau! Cuba; Martinique; d'Orb.!

C. litteratum Brug. station: young specimens dredged
from 9 fathoms water on blue sandy mud; habitat:
Cuba; Sagra! Auber! Martinique; Guadeloupe; Candé!
Carthagena; Bermuda; Redfield! Jamaica; Ad.! St. Thomas; Tortola; St. Martin; Barbados; Trinidad; Krebs!

C. megasoma Ad. station: — ? — ; habitat: Jamaica; Ad.! remark: described in „Contributions" No
7. April 1850 page 119.

C. mirabile Ad. station: — ? —; habitat: Jamaica;
Adams! remark: described in the 7te „contribution"
page 118.

C. muscarum Say. station: Jamaica; Ad.! Cuba; Florida; d'Orb.!

C. mutabile Ad. station: — ? —; habitat: Jamaica;
Ad.! remark: described in „Proc. of the Boston Soc. of
N. Hist." 1st January 1845 page 5.

C. minimum Gml. (C. zonale Brug.) station: on rocks
in the surface of the water close to the shore and on
the beach where there is coarse gravel; only where the
sea is calm; habitat: Curaçao; Mörch! St. Thomas;
Tortola; Carthagena; Krebs! remark: it varies very
much and several shells described as separate species
will in the future be shown to be synonymes with this.

C. nigrescens Mk. station: on rocks in the surface of
the water along the shore; habitat: Guadeloupe; Petit!
Beau! St. Thomas; St. Johns; Jamaica; Florida; Ad.!

St. Thomas; St. Martha; Carthagena; Krebs! remark:
it is surely synonyme with C. septemstriatum Say. and
perhaps with C. minimum Gml.

C. ornatum Dnk. station: —? —; habitat: Antillae;
Mörch!

C. Petitii Kien. station: —? —; habitat: St. Croix;
Saba; R. Swift! Guadeloupe; Duchassain! Porto-Plata;
St. Martin; Krebs!

C. punctatum L. (according to Beau: C. subulatum Montf.
C. Emersonii C B. Ad.!) station: —? —; habitat:
Guadeloupe; Beau! Duchassain! St. Thomas; Porto-
Plata; Krebs!

C. rugulosum Ad. station: — ? —; habitat: Jamaica; Ad.! St. Thomas; St. Johns; St. Martin; Krebs!

C. scalariforme Say. station: —? —; habitat: Jamaica; E. Chitty! Florida; Ad.!

C. Sagra d'Orb. station: — ? —; habitat: Cuba;
Auber!

C. semiferrugineum Lmk. station: — ? —; habitat: Guadeloupe; Beau! St. Thomas; St. Martin; Krebs!
remark: a variety of C. litteratum Brug.

C. septemstriatum Say. station: — ? —; habitat:
Bahama; Ad.! remark: see C. nigrescens Mnk.

C. terebellum Ad. station: — ? —; habitat: Jamaica; Ad.! St. Thomas; St. Martin; Pto.-Plata; Krebs!

C. versicolor Ad. station: — ? —; habitat: Jamaica; Ad.! Guadeloupe; Beau! St. Thomas; Bland!
remark: described in C. B. Ad. „Contribution" No 7
page 119. April 1850.

C. variabile Ad. station: —? —; habitat: Jamaica;
Ad.! remark: described in „Proc. of the Boston Soc.
of N. Hist." 1st January 1854.

C. vicinum Ad. station: — ? —; habitat: Jamaica;
Ad! remark: described in 7te „Contribution" of C. B.
Adams page 122.

Triforis Deshayes.

T. dealbatus Ad. station: — ? —; habitat: Jamaica;
Ad! remark! described in „Contribution" No 7 page
117. April 1850.

T. decoratus Ad. station: — ? —; habitat: Jamaica;
Ad.! remark: described in „Contribution" No 7 page
117. April 1850.

T. exiguus Ad. station: — ? —; habitat: Jamaica;
Ad.! remark: described in „Contribution" No 7 page
118. April 1850.

T. intermedius Ad. station: — ? — ; habitat: Jamaica; Ad.! remark: described in „Contribution" No
7 page 119. April 1850.

T. melanura Ad. station: — ? —; habitat: Jamaica;
Ad.! remark: described in „Contribution" No 7 page
117. April 1850.

T. mirabilis Ad. station: — ? —; habitat: St. Johns;
Jamaica; Ad.! remark: described in „Contribution" No
7 page 118. April 1850.

T. modestus Ad. station: — ? —; habitat: Jamaica;
Ad.! remark: described in „Contribution" No 7 page
117. April 1850.

T. nanus Ad. station: — ? — ; habitat: Jamaica;
Ad.! remark: described in „Contribution" No 7 page
117. April 1850.

T. ornatus Desh. (Hinds according to Beau) station: — ?
— ; habitat: Jamaica; Ad.! Guadeloupe; Beau! St.
Thomas; St. Croix; Krebs!

T. pulchellus Ad. station: — ? — ; habitat: Jamaica; St. Thomas; Ad.! remark: described in „Contribution" No 7 page 121. April 1850.

T. turris Thomae d'Orb. station: — ? — ; habitat: Cuba; Guadeloupe; d'Orb.! Guadeloupe; Beau!

Paludinacea.

Litiopa Rang.

L. effusa Ad. station: — ? — ; habitat: Jamaica; Ad.! remark: described in „Contribution" No 5 page 71.

L. maculata Rang. station: On seaweed in the gulfstream Ad.! habitat: Jamaica; Cuba; d'Orbig.! St. Thomas; Krebs!

L. obesa Ad. station: — ? — ; habitat: Jamaica; Ad.! St. Thomas; Krebs! remark: described in the „Contribution" No 5 page 71; the nucleus of this species is strongly costulated like that of L. mac. R.

L. striata Pf. station: on sea-weed; Ad.! habitat: in the gulfstream; Ad.!

Planaxis Lamarck.

P. nucleus Lmk. station: on rocks between high and low water mark; habitat: Martinique; Guadeloupe; St. Lucy; Cuba; Auber! Candé! Beau! Jamaica; Ad.! St. Thomas; Sta. Martha; St. Johns; St. Martin; Anguilla; Krebs!

P. lineatus Da Costa (P. pedicularis Lmk.) station: on rocks and in hollows between high and low water mark; habitat: Antillae; Mörch! England; Da Costa! Java; Lmk.! St. Vincent (Canary-Islands); Schmidt! Jamaica; Ad.! Guadeloupe; Petit! Beau! St. Johns; St. Martin; St. Thomas; Krebs!

Rissoa Flemingville (Cingula; Alvania).

R. aberrans Ad. station: — ? —; habitat: Jamaica; Ad.! Vieques; A. H. Riise! remark: described in „Contribution" No 7 page 113.

R. affinis Ad. station: — ? —; habitat: Jamaica; Ad.! remark: described in „proceedings of the Boston Soc. of Nat. hist." 1st January 1845 page 6.

R. albida Ad. (Rissoina acc. to von Möhrenberg) station: — ? —; habitat: Jamaica; Ad.! St. Thomas; A. H. Riise! remark: described in „Proceed. of the Boston Soc. of Nat. History." 1st January 1845 page 6.

R. Auberiana d'Orb. station: dead in the sand of the beach; habitat: Cuba; Sagra! St. Thomas; Jamaica; Candé! St. Thomas; Krebs! remark: described in „Mollusques de Cuba". 2d. part, page 22.

R. canaliculata (Odostomia) Ad. station: — ? —; habitat: Jamaica; Ad.!

R. caribaea d'Orb. station: dead in the sand of the beach; habitat: Jamaica; de Candé! Cuba; Sagra! remark: described in „Mollusques de Cuba" part 2 page 21.

R. carinata Recluz. station: — ? —; habitat: St. Thomas! A. H. Riise!

R. chesnellii v. major Mich. station: — ? —; habitat: Cuba; A. H. Riise!

R. concinna (Cingula) Ad. station: — ? —; habitat: Jamaica; Ad.! remark: described in the „Contribution" No 5 page 70.

R. conica (Cingula?) Ad. station: — ? —; habitat: Jamaica; Ad.! remark: described in „Contribution" No 5 page 70.

R. crassicosta Ad. station: — ? —; habitat: Jamaica; Ad.! remark: described in „Proc. of the Boston Soc. of Nat. History". 1st January 1845 page 6.

R. dubiosa Ad. station: — ? —; habitat: Jamaica; Ad.! St. Thomas; Th. Bland! remark: described in „Contributions" No 7 page 114.

R. culimoides Ad. station: — ? — ; habitat: Jamaica; Ad.! remark: described in „Contribution" No 7 page 115.

R. gemmulosa (Odostomia) Ad. station: —? — ; habitat: Jamaica; Ad!

R. gradata d'Orb. station: in the sand of the beach; habitat: Jamaica; d'Orb.! remark: described in „Mollusque de Cuba" part 2d. page 23.

R. laevigata Ad. (Rissoina; Möhrenstern) station: — ? —; habitat: Jamaica; Ad.! St. Thomas; A. H. Riise! remark: described in „Contribution" No 7 page 114.

R. laevissima Ad. (Rissoina; Möhrenstern) station: —? — ; habitat: Jamaica; Ad.! St. Thomas; Bland! A. H. Riise! remark: described in „Contribution" No 5 page 115.

R. melanura Ad. station: —? —; habitat: Jamaica; Ad.! St. Thomas; A. H. Riise! Guadeloupe; Trinidad; St. Martin; St. Croix; St. Thomas; Krebs! remark: we agree with C. B. Adams, who has described this species in „Contribution" No 8 page 116, that it is not a Rissoa and we take it to be the shell described by d'Orbigny as Eulima incerta, but he himself doubts it is an Eulima; we doubt it to be eather a Rissoa or an Eulima; we have specimens with two and three strongly eveloped varices on each whorl and in some few specimens are the varices forming two or three continuous rows from the, in the most cases, black nucleus until the last whorl.

R. multicostata Ad. station: — ? — ; habitat: Jamaica; Ad.! remark: described in the „Contribution" No 7 page 114, in which Ad. refers to Rissoina elegantissima d'Orb., with which we consider it synonyme — Professor C. B. Adams, who has contributed so much to the evelopment of the natural history of the West-Indies and who, by his practical way of collecting and arranging as he collected, has done more for the knowledge of the geographical destribution of the marine shells on both sides of the american continent, than any man of science before him, had quite a sickly passion for describing „supposed new shells", by which he, as well as many of his contemporaries, has confused and burthened the science with innumerable synonymes, which men of science in future days will have trouble to find through.

R. ovuloides (Odostomia) Ad. station: — ? — ; habitat: Jamaica; Ad.!

R. princeps Ad. station: — ? — ; habitat: Jamaica; Ad.! remark: described in his „Contribution" No 7 page 116. where he says it is allied to R. albida Ad.

R. pulchra Ad. (Rissoina acc. to Möhrenberg) station: — ? — ; habitat: Jamaica; Ad.! St. Thomas; Th. Bland! A. H. Riise! St. Barth; Krebs! remark: described by C. B. Adams in „Contribution" No 7 page 114; very near allied to Rissoina Sagraina d'Orb.! and Rissoa cancellata Phil.

R. pusilla Desh. station: — ? — ; habitat: Cuba; A. H. Riise!

R. solida (Odostomia) Ad. station: — ? — ; habitat:

Jamaica; Ad.! remark: he describes it in „Contribution" No 5 page 70 as Cingula solida.

R. scalarella Ad. (Rissoina Möhrenberg) station: — ?
— ; habitat: Jamaica; Ad.! St. Thomas; Th. Bland!
A. H. Riise! remark: described in „Proc. of the Boston S. of Natural History." 1st January 1845. see Rissoina Catesbya d'Orbigny and „Contribution" No 7 page
113.

R. scalaroides Ad. (Rissoina Möhrenberg) station: — ?
— ; habitat: Jamaica; Ad.! St. Thomas; A. II. Riise!
remark: described in „Contribution" No 7 page 113;
by Philippi considered a Rissoina; see Zeitschrifft 1848
page 13.

R. scalaroides minor Ad. station: — ? — ; habitat: Jamaica; Ad.! remark: described in „Contribution" No 7 page 113.

R. striosa Ad. station: in sand on the beach; Ad.!
habitat: Jamaica; Ad.! St. Thomas; Th. Bland! remark: described in „Contribution" No 7 page 116.

R. subangulata Ad. station: — ? — ; habitat: Jamaica; Ad.! remark: described in „Contribution" No 7
page 112.

R. trivaricosa Ad. station: — ? — ; habitat: Jamaica; Ad.! St. Croix; A. II. Riise! remark: described
in „Proc. of Boston Soc. of Natural History." 1st January 1845 page 6. see R. melanura Ad.

R. umbilicata Ph. station: — ? — ; habitat: St.
Thomas; A. II. Riise!

R. vitrea Ad. station: — ? — ; habitat: Jamaica;
Ad.! remark: described in „Contribution" No 7 page
113.

Rissoina d'Orbigny.

R. albida Ad. station: — ? —; habitat: St. Thomas;
A. H. Riise!

R. Browniana d'Orb. station: In sand on the beach;
habitat: St. Thomas; Haity; Martinique; de Candé!
St. Thomas & St. Johns; Krebs! remark: described in
„Mollusques de Cuba" 2 part, page 28.

R. cancellata Ph. station: dead in the sand on the
beach; habitat: Cuba; Pfeiffer! remark: described in
Zeitschrift 1847 page 127.

R. Catesbya d'Orb. station: dead in the white sand on
the beach and life on dead madrepores laying on the
beach between high and low water mark; habitat:
Cuba; Sagra! St. Thomas; R. Swift! Martinique; St.
Thomas; Haity; Candé! Portoplata; St. Thomas; St.
Croix; St. Johns; St. Martin; Krebs! Guadeloupe; Beau!
St. Thomas; A. H. Riise! remark: This R. Cat. d'Orb.
is certainly the same as the shell A. H. Riise Esq. has
in his Collection by the name of Rissoa Dunkeri Pf. and
we consider it the same shell as C. B. Adams Rissoa
scalaroides, R. scalaroides minor and R. scalarella. The
number of ribs and their proportion are very variable;
we have a large number of specimens before us and we
have come to the conclusion that they are one species.

R. decussata Montg. station: — ? — ; habitat: St.
Thomas; A. H. Riise!

R. dubiosa C. B. Ad. station: — ? —; habitat: St.
Thomas; A. H. Riise!

R. elegantissima d'Orb. station: only found dead in
the sand on the beach; habitat: Haity; d'Orbig.! St.
Martin; Anguilla; Krebs! remark: Described in „Mollusques de Cuba" part 2, page 26.

R. Phillippiana Pheiff. station: — ? — ; habitat: Viegnes; Cuba; A. H. Riise!

R. reticulata Sowb. station: — ? — ; habitat: St. Thomas; A. H. Riise!

R. Sagraina d'Orb. station: — ? — ; habitat: Martinique; St. Thomas; Candé! remark: described in „Mollusque de Cuba" part 2d. page 25. See Rissoa pulchra Ad.

R. scalariformis Ad. station: —? — ; habitat: St. Thomas; A. H. Riise!

R. scalaroides see Rissoa scalaroides Ad. and Rissoina Catesbya d'Orb.!

R. Sloania d'Orb. station: only found dead in the sand of the beach; habitat: Jamaica; Candé! remark: described in „Mollusques de Cuba" part 2 page 28.

R. striato-costata d'Orb. station: dead in the sand of the beach; habitat: Cuba; Sagra Haity; Candé! St. Barth; Passage – Island near St. Thomas; Porto - Plata; Krebs! remark: described in „Mollusques de Cuba" part 2d page 27.

Fossarus Adans.

F. sulcatus d'Orb. station: — ? — ; habitat: Guadeloupe: Beau! remark: we are of opinion it is a young Narica.

Littorina Ferussac.

L. angulifera Lmk. (Littorina scabra d'Orb.) station: Always on Mangletrees; d'Orb.! On bulwarks and old wood close to the shore; Krebs! habitat: Brasils; Mörch! All the Antilles; Jamaica; d'Orb.! Cuba; Sagra! Martinique; Guadeloupe; Rang! Candé! Saint Cur. Hotessier! St. Thomas; St. Johns; St. Croix; Portorico; Jamaica; Krebs!

L. Antonii Phil. station: — ? —; habitat: Jamaica; Ad.! St. Thomas; Th. Bland! Antilles; Mörch!

L. carinata d'Orb. Moll. de Cuba 1. 209; station: — ? — ; habitat: Havana; Sagra! Auber! Martinique; Candé! Rang! Antilles; Mörch! remark: d'Orbigny observes that those at Martinique are smaller than those at Havana. It would be very interesting to study if a species has a centre where the individuals evelope them-selves to the greatest size and to the highest degree of perfection and from there toward the radius decrease in size and perfection. Several series of shells in our col-lection alove us to cherish this idea.

L. columellaris d'Orb. station: On rocks; Beau! ha-bitat: Pernambuco; d'Orb.! Martinique; Candé! Point à Pitre; Guadeloupe; Beau! Cat. pg. 12; Havana; K. Prescot! remark: Described in „Mollusques de Cuba" p. 1 p. 213.

L. Gundlachi Ph. station: — ? —; habitat: Cuba; Gundlach! remark: Described in „Zeitschrift" 1848—150.

L. guttata Ph. (L. punctata Pf.) station: Found on poles in quiet water, close to the beach; habitat: Antilles; Mörch! Guadeloupe; Petit! Beau! Duchassain! St. Tho-mas; Bland! Jamaica; Ad.! St. Thomas; St. Johns; St. Martin; Porto-Plata and Carthagena (N. Gr.); Krebs!

L. dilatata d'Orb. station: — ? —; habitat: Havana; Sagra! Auber! K. Prescott! Florida; Alphen|! Porto-Plata; Krebs! Jamaica; Ad.! remark: Described in „Mollusques de Cuba" 1—207.

L. flava Brod. (L. irrorata var. Petit) station: — ? —; habitat: Brasils (?); Ad.! Guadeloupe; Petit!

L. lineata d'Orb. station: On rocks; Beau! Especielly in small caves on the rocks between high and low-water mark; Krebs! habitat: Havana; Sagra! Auber! Martinique; Candé! Rio Janeiro; d'Orbigny! Guadeloupe; Beau! Duchassain! St. Thomas; Th. Bland! Krebs! St. Johns; E. Hartwig! Krebs! Jamaica; Ad.! Arecibo; J. H. Newton! St. Martin; Porto-Plata; Chagres; Krebs! remark: Described in „Mollusque de Cuba" 1—208. Those d'Orbigny had received from Martinique were the largest, those next were from Havana and the smallest from Rio Janeiro; the largest we have are from St. Thomas the smallest from Porto-Plata.

L. jamaicensis Ad. station: — ? — ; habitat: Jamaica; Ad.! remark: Described in „Contribution" No 5 page 71.

L. minima Wood. station: Very common on the poles of the wharfs; Beau! habitat: West-Indies; S. Hovey! Antilles; Mörch! Guadeloupe; Beau! St. Martin; Krebs! St. Croix; Riise!

L. muricata Linné (Tectus muricatus Ch.? gothicus Bolt?) station: On rocks always over high water mark; habitat: Antillae; Mörch! Cuba; Sagra! Auber! Martinique; Candé! St. Lucy and Florida; d'Orbigny! Guadeloupe; Beau! St. Martin; St. Thomas; Krebs!

L. mespilum Mode. (L. fusca Pfr. according to C. B. Adams) station: — ? — ; habitat: Jamaica & Florida; Ad.! Havana; K. Prescott!

L. naticoides d'Orbig. station: — ? — ; habitat: Havana; Sagra! Auber! remark: Described in „Moll. de Cuba" 1—214.

L. nodulosa Gml. station: — ? — ; habitat: Martinique; Candé! St. Lucy! d'Orbig.! Jamaica; Ad.! Arecibo;

J. H. Newton! Havana; K. Prescott! remark: Described
in „Moll. de Cuba" 1—205.

L. nodulosa Ph. station: — ? — ; habitat: Guadeloupe; Beau!

L. d'Orbigniana Phil. station: — ? — ; habitat:
Guadeloupe; Beau! Cat. pg. 12; Carthagena (New Gr.);
Krebs!

L. scabra Linné. station: — ? — ; habitat: Guadeloupe; Beau! Mörch! 46. Ind. orient. d'Orbig. 1 Moll.
de Cuba pg. 212.

L. tesselata Phil. station: — ? — ; habitat: Jamaica;
Ad.! St. Johns; E. Hartwig! Guadeloupe; Beau! Cat.
pg. 12.

L. tigrina d'Orb. station: In clusters on wood laying
on the beach between high & low water mark; habitat:
Havana; Sagra! Auber! Guadeloupe; Saint Cyr Hotessier!
Chagres; Krebs! remark: Those we found at Chagres
were, with exception of one specimen, of a uniform pale
colour.

L. trochiformis Dillw. (L. nodulosa d'Orb. acc. to Beau)
station: — ? — ; habitat: Guadeloupe; Beau! St.
Martin; Krebs! Jamaica; Ad.! Havana; K. Prescott!
Tortola; E. Hartwig!

L. tuberculata d'Orb. (L. nodulosa Ph. acc. to Beau)
station: On rocks; d'Orb.! habitat: Cuba; Sagra!
Auber! Porto-Plata; Krebs! Guadeloupe; Beau! remark:
Described in „Moll. de Cuba" 1. 206.

L. undulata d'Orb. station: — ? — ; habitat: Martinique; Candé! remark: Described in „Moll. de Cuba"
1—212.

L. ziczac Chem. station: In crevices of the rocks between high and low water mark; Krebs! on the coast;

Beau! habitat: Antilles; Mörch. pag. 46! Havana;
Sagra! Auber! Martinique; Candé! Guadeloupe; Beau.
Cat. pg. 12! St. Thomas; Krebs! Th. Bland! E. Hart-
wig; Barbados; Chemnitz! Lmk.! Jamaica; Ad.! Arecibo;
J. H. Newton! Carthagena (N. Gr.); Redfield!

Modulus Gray.

M. lenticularis Ch. (Trochus unidens List d'Orb.) sta-
tion: On sandy mud about 2 to 4 feet water, especielly
on sea-weed; habitat: St. Thomas; St. Martin; St.
Barth; Guadeloupe; St. Martha; Carthagena; Krebs!
Cuba; Sagra! Auber! Martinique; Candé! Guadeloupe;
Hotessier! Petit! Beau! Florida; d'Orb.! Ad.! St. Johns;
E. Hartwig! St. Thomas; Th. Bland! Carthagena; Red-
field; Jamaica; Ad.! Antillae; Mörch pag. 45!

M. perlatus. station: On plants close to the coast;
Krebs! habitat: Carthagena N. G.; Krebs! remark:
Descidedly different from the former.

M. — ? station: — ? — ; habitat: Virgin-Islands;
Krebs!

Solarium Lmk.

S. aethiops Menke. station: —? —; habitat: Puertorico; Philippi! remark: Described in „Zeitschrift"
1848 page 167.

S. bisulcatum d'Orb. (Euomphalus Sowb.?) station:
Dead in sand on the beach; habitat: Jamaica; Martinique; d'Orb.! Jamaica; Ad.! Arecibo; J. H. Newton!
remark: Described in „Moll. de Cuba" 2 part 66.

S. delphinuloides d'Orb. station: Found in sand; habitat: Jamaica; d'Orb.! remark: Described in „Moll.
de Cuba" 2—67.

S. granulatum Lmk. station: — ? — ; habitat: Guadeloupe; Hotessier! Cuba; d'Orb.! Haity; Mazatlan; (?Kr.) Menke! Jamaica; Ad.! Carthagena; St. Martha; Porto-Plata; Krebs! remark: The young specimens are perfectly smooth on the surface.

S. Herbertii Dh. (Heliacus d'Orb. Tr. cylindraceus Chem. Tr. cylindricus Gml.) station; Inserted in slimy zoophytes on rocks about low - water mark; habitat: Cuba; Auber! Jamaica; Ad.! St. Thomas; Krebs! Guadeloupe; Beau! Hotessier! Antillae; Mörch pag. 47!

S. infundibuliformis Chem. (Tr. Chemnitzii Ki.) station: — ? — ; habitat: Porto-Plata; St. Thomas; St. Martin; Krebs! Antillae Mörch pag. 47!

S. inornatum d'Orb. station: In sand; habitat: St. Thomas; Candé! remark: Described in „Moll. de Cuba" 2—67.

S. nubilum Menke. station: — ? — ; habitat: Cap. Haity; Philippi!

Scalariacea.

Scalaria Lamarck.

S. albida d'Orb. (Sc. fragilis Hanl. acc. to Beau) station: — ? — ; habitat: Cuba; Auber! Guadeloupe; Beau! remark: Should this not be Sowerby's Scalaria tenuis?

S. Candeana d'Orbig. station: — ? — ; habitat: Jamaica & St. Thomas; Candé! remark: The specimens described by d'Orbigny were found dead in the sand on the beach.

S. coronata Lmk. station: — ? — ; habitat: Guadeloupe! Beau pg. 12!

S. crenata Linné. station: — ? — ; habitat: Jamaica; Ad.! Arecibo; J. H. Newton! St. Thomas; St. Martin;

Anguilla; Krebs! remark: See our remark on Sc. Hotesseriana d'Orbig.

S. denticulata Sowb. station: — ? — ; habitat: West-Indies; Jay's cat.! Guadeloupe; Beau!

S. echinaticosta d'Orb. station: The specimen described found in the sand on the beach; habitat: St. Thomas; d'Orbig.! Krebs! R. Swift!

S. foliaccicostata d'Orb. station: — ? — ; habitat: Guadeloupe; Beau! Martinique; Guadeloupe; St. Thomas; Candé! Anguilla; St. Thomas; Porto-Plata; Krebs! remark: Described in „Moll. de Cuba" 2—12.

S. fragilis Hanley. station: — ? — ; habitat: Guadeloupe; Petit! Jamaica; Ad.!

S. Hotesseriana d'Orb. station: — ? — ; habitat: Guadeloupe; Hotessier! Beau pg. 12! St. Martin; Porto-Plata; Krebs! remark: Take d'Orbigny's drawing of S. Hot. and Lamarcks description of Scalaria crenata Linné; they approach surely each other very much.

S. lamellosa Lmk. (Scl. clathrus Linné acc. to Beau) station: Young specimens found on pieces of dead madrepores in a depth of water of 3 feet; habitat: Seas of Europe; Lamarck! St. Thomas; Th. Bland! St. Johns; J. Mac-Murry! Jamaica; Ad.! Cuba; Auber! Guadeloupe; St. Lucy; Hotessier! Candé! St. Thomas; St. Johns; Passage-Island; St. Martin; Anguilla; Guadeloupe; Krebs! Guadeloupe; Beau pag. 12!

S. lineata Say. station: — ? — ; habitat: West-Indies; according to a note in Amherst Museum! Guadeloupe; Beau pag. 12!

S. ligata Ad. station: — ? — ; habitat: Jamaica; Ad.! remark: Described in Contribution No 4 page 67. January 1850.

S. Martini Wood? station: — ? — ; habitat: St. Barth; St. Martin; Krebs!

S. modesta Ad. station: — ? — ; habitat: Jamaica; Ad.! Porto Cabello; R. Swift! remark: S. venosa Sowb. is according to Jay's Catalogue synonyme with this species.

S. muricata Kur. station: — ? — ; habitat: Florida; Ad.! St. Thomas; Th. Bland! Guadeloupe; Petit!

S. pernobilis Fisch. & Bern. station: — ? — ; habitat: Marie Galante; Beau!

S. tenuis Sowb. station: — ? — ; habitat: St. Thomas; Th. Bland! St. Thomas; St. Johns; St. Croix; St. Martin; Barbados; Trinidad; Porto - Plata; Krebs! Guadeloupe; Beau pg. 12!

S. uncinaticosta d'Orb. station: — ? — ; habitat: Guadeloupe; Candé! Beau pg. 12! St. Thomas; Krebs! R. Swift! remark: Described in „Moll. de Cuba" 2—19.

S. varicosa Lmk. station: In mud on 1 to 2 feet water; habitat: Tortola; R. Swift! St. Croix; H. Krebs!

Ianthinacea.

Ianthina Lamarck.

I. exigua Lmk. station: — ? — ; habitat: Guadeloupe; Beau!

I. fragilis Ad. station: — ? — ; habitat: Jamaica; Ad.!

I. globosa Sow. station: — ? — ; habitat: Jamaica; Ad.!

I. planispira Reeve. station: floating on shore on sandy beaches; habitat: St. Thomas; A. H. Riise! Guadeloupe; Beau! St. Thomas & St. Johns; Krebs!

I. prolongata Blainville. station: — ? — ; habitat: Cuba; d'Orb.! Jamaica; Ad.!

I. umbilicata d'Orb. station: — ? — ; habitat: Cuba; d'Orb.! remark: Described in 2d. part page 85 in mollusques de Cuba.

Stylina Fleming.

S. subulata Brod. station: Found dead in holes bored by Littophages in madrepores: habitat: St. Thomas; Th. Bland! R. Swift! J. Knox! St. Thomas; St. Croix; St. Martin; Krebs!

Naticacea.

Natica Adanson.

N. canrena L. station: On sand 4 to 6 feet under water ot a certain season of the year (Nov. De?) habitat: West-Indies Mörch 1—134! Brasils; Cuba; Martinique; St. Lucy; Guadeloupe; Florida; d'Orb.! Jamaica; Turks-Island; Bermuda; Ad.! St. Barth; St. Thomas; St. Johns; Tortola; Anguilla; St. Martin; Krebs! Guadeloupe; Beau!

N. fuscata Chem. (N. brunnea Link. N. mamilaris) station: In the clear sand 4 to 5 feet from the shore i Great Northside Bay at St. Thomas; habitat: West-Indies; Mörch pag. 132! Cuba; St. Lucy; d'Orb.! Jamaica; Navy-Bay; Carthagena; Ad.! Guadeloupe; Beau! Trinidad; Jamaica; St. Thomas; St. Martin; Porto-Plata; Carthagena; Krebs!

N. Lacernula d'Orb. station: — ? — ; habitat: Martinique; Candé! Cuba; de la Sagra! remark: see Moll. de Cuba 2. 35.

N. **lactea** Ph. station: lives in sand; habitat: St. Thomas; Krebs! remark: the epidermis is gray.

N. **marochiensis** ? Lmk. station: —? — ; habitat Guadeloupe; Beau!

N. **Menkeana** Pfr. station: —? — ; habitat: Puertoricco; Zeitsch. 1851 pg. 46! West-Indies; Krebs!

N. **nitida** Donovan (N. mamilla L. Naticina lactea Guild.) station: —? —; habitat: West-Indies; Mörch pag. 132! St. Thomas; Tortola; Barbados; Krebs! Cuba; Martinique; Guadeloupe; St. Lucy; d'Orb. 2. 32! St. Thomas; Tortola; Jamaica; Cuba; Carthagena; Ad.!

N. **ochrostoma** Recluz. station: —? — ; habitat: West-Indies? remark: Journal de Coch. 1850 pg. 391.

N. **Pfeiferi** Ph. station: —? — ; habitat: St. Thomas. ?; Krebs! remark: Very like Natica lactea Ph. but the epidermis is yellowish-brown; perhaps only a variety.

N. **proxima** Ad. station: —? —; habitat: Jamaica; Tortola; Arecibo; St. Croix; C. B. Ad.! St. Thomas; St. Johns; Barbados; Porto-Plata; Krebs! remark: By us considered young Nat. canrena L.

N. **pulchella** Pfr. (N. jamaicensis Ad. N. Sagriana d'Orb.) station: —? — ; habitat: Jamaica; Turks-Island; Ad.! St. Thomas; Anguilla; Trinidad; Krebs! Cuba; Sagra! d'Orb. 2. 34. of Moll. de Cuba.

N. **pusilla** Say. station: —? — ; habitat: Guadeloupe; Beau!

N. **rugosa** Chem. (N. cancellata Gml.) station: —? —; habitat: Guadeloupe; Beau! West-Indies; Mörch pag. 133! St. Johns; Ad.! St. Johns; Porto-Plata; St. Croix; Trinidad; Krebs!

N. **sulcata** Born. (Natica rugosa Gml. N. costata Mke.)

station: — ? — ; habitat: West-Indies; Mörch pag.
133! Cuba; Auber! remark: we believe it is synonyme
with N. rugosa Chem.

Sigaretus Lamarck.

S. depressus Philippi (S. antillarum Recluz) station:
— ? — ; habitat: West-Indies; Mörch pag. 131! Cuba;
St. Lucy; d'Orb.! Guadeloupe; Beau! St. Thomas; Tortola; Krebs!

S. haliotideus. station: — ? —; habitat: Jamaica;
C. B. Adams!

S. maculatus Say. station: — ? —; habitat: Jamaica
& St. Johns; C. B. Adams!

S. zonatus d'Orb. (S. martinianus Ph.) station: — ? —;
habitat: West-Indies; Mörch pg. 131! Guadeloupe;
Hotessier! Beau! St. Thomas; St. Martin; Krebs!

Naricaceæ.
Narica Recluz.

N. granulosa Recluz. station: — ? —; habitat: St.
Thomas; Krebs!

N. lamellosa d'Orb. station: — ? —; habitat: Cuba;
Martinique; Guadeloupe; Candé! Guadeloupe; Beau! St.
Johns; St. Barth; Anguilla; Porto-Plata; Krebs!

N. striata d'Orb. station: — ? — ; habitat: Cuba;
Auber!

N. sulcata d'Orb. station: — ? —; habitat: Havana;
Auber! St. Lucy; Jamaica; de Candé!

Xenophorea.
Xenophora Fischer von Waldheim.

X. trochiformis Born. (Onustus Humph. Phorus Mtf.)

station: in 8 to 10 feet water on sand; habitat: St. Thomas; Mörch pg. 49! Martinique; Candé! Guadeloupe; Beau! St. Thomas; Tortola; Porto-Plata; St. Croix; St. Johns; Krebs!

X. caribæa Petit. station: — ? — ; habitat: Marie-Galante; Beau!

Calyptraeacea.

Crucibulum Schumacher.

(Calypeopsis Les. Dispotea Say).

C. auriculatum Ch. (P. auriculata Gml.) station: — ? — ; habitat: West-Indies; Mörch pag. 146! St. Thomas; St. Croix; Anguilla; St. Martin; St. Barth; Guadeloupe; Barbados; Puertoricco; Porto-Plata; Krebs!

C. radiata Brod. station: — ? — ; habitat: Caracas; Mörch pag. 146! (La Guyra?) St. Thomas; Tortola; St. Croix; Krebs!

Mitrularia Schumacher.

M. esqvestris Lmk. station: — ? — ; habitat: Africa; l'île de Prince; Cuba; Florida; d'Orb.! East-Indies; Mörch! remark: Is confounded by d'Orbigny and others with Crucibulum auriculatum Chem.

Trochita Schumacher. (Infundibulum d'Orb.)

T. candeana d'Orb. station: — ? — ; habitat: St. Domingo; Jamaica; St. Thomas; Martinique; de Candé! Cuba; Sagra! Porto-Plata; St. Thomas; St. Martin; Anguilla; Krebs! St. Thomas; R. Swift!

Crepidula Lamarck.

C. aculeata Chem. station: On dead Madrepores laying

in 2 feet water; habitat: West-Indies; Mörch pg. 147! Cuba; Patagonia; Brasils; Guadeloupe; d'Orb.! Guadeloupe; Beau! Jamaica; Ad.! St. Thomas; St. Johns; St. Croix; Krebs!

C. fornicata Lmk. station: — ? — ; habitat: Barbadoes; Lamarck!

C. protea d'Orb. station: Found on Strombus pugillis; habitat: Patagonia; Brasils; Cuba; d'Orbig.! Guadeloupe; Beau! St. Thomas; Porto-Plata; Krebs!

C. Riisei Dnk. station: — ? — ; habitat: St. Juan de Puertorico; Riise!

C. unguiformis Lmk. (C. plana Say acc. to C. B. Ad.!) station: — ? — ; habitat: Guadeloupe; Beau! Jamaica & Carthagena; C. B. Ad.! remark: We think the C. fornicata, C. protea and C. auguiformis are synonymes; they appear under very different shape and colours.

Capulus D. Montfort (Hipponyx).

C. antiqvatus L. (P. mitrula Gm. — P. cernua Spr.) station: — ? — ; habitat: West-Indies; Mörch! Guadeloupe; Beau! Cuba; de la Sagra! Florida; d'Orb.! Martinique; Guadeloupe; St. Lucy; Candé! Hotessier!

C. incurvus Gm. (P. militaris L., Dw., P. intorta Lmk.) station: — ? —; habitat: West-Indies? Mörch pg. 145! Cuba; Guadeloupe; d'Orb. 2. 187! Guadeloupe; Beau! St. Thomas; St. Croix; St. Martin; St. Barth; Guadeloupe; Barbadoes; Porto-Plata; Krebs!

C. pilosa Desh. station: — ? — ; habitat: Guadeloupe; Beau!

C. subrufa Mart. station: — ? — ; habitat: West-Indies; Mörch pg. 145! Cuba; Sagra! Guadeloupe; Beau!

Porto-Plata; Guadeloupe; Krebs! remark: Moll. de
Cuba; d'Orb. p. 2. pg. 187 pl. 24. fig. 24—25.

C. trigona Gml. — ? —; habitat: West-Indies; Mörch
pag. 45!

Ringiculacea.

Cinulia Gray.

C. semistriata d'Orb. station: — ? — ; habitat:
Jamaica; Candé! remark: Described in d'Orbigny's Moll.
de Cuba 2. 103. pl. 31—$\frac{17}{19}$.

Pyramidellacea.

Pyramidella Lamarck.

P. dolabrata L. station: — ? — ; habitat: West-
Indies; Mörch pg. 45! Cuba; Sagra! Guadeloupe & St.
Lucy; Hotessier! Guadeloupe; Beau! St. Thomas; St.
Jan; Crabisland; Portoplata; St. Martin; Anguilla; Krebs!

P. terebellum Lmk. station: — ? — ; habitat: Jamaica; E. Chitty! St. Johns; Jamaica; Bermuda; Ad.!

Odontostoma Fleming.

O. depressa d'Orb. station: — ? —; habitat: Cuba;
Sagra! remark: Described in d'Orb. Moll. de Cuba
1—238.

O. globosa d'Orb. station: — ? — ; habitat: Cuba;
d'Orb.! remark: Described in d'Orb. Moll. de Cuba
1—239.

O. pusilla (Pyramidella) Pfef. station: — ? — ; habitat: Cuba; Zeitschrift 1851. pg. 88.

Monostygma Gray.

1 spec-indet. St. Thomas; Krebs!

Turbonilla Risso (Chemnitzia).

T. **babylonia** Ad. station: — ? — ; habitat: Jamaica; Ad.!

T. **cancellata** d'Orb. station: — ? — ; habitat: Cuba; Sagra! remark: Described by d'Orb. in Moll. de Cuba 1—225. pl. 17. fig. 1—3.

T. **dubia** d'Orb. station: — ? — ; habitat: Jamaica; Guadeloupe; Martinique; St. Thomas; Cuba; Rio Janeiro; d'Orb.! Guadeloupe; Beau! remark: Described by d'Orb. in „Moll. de Cuba" 1. 226. pl. 17 fig. 4—6.

T. **elegans** d'Orb. station: — ? — ; habitat: Guadeloupe; de Candé! Beau! remark: Described by d'Orb. in „Moll. de Cuba" 1—223. pl. 16. fig. 25. 27.

T. **exilis** Ad. station: — ? — ; habitat: Jamaica; Ad.!

T. **flavocincta** Ad. station: — ? — ; habitat: Jamaica; Ad.!

T. **laevigata** d'Orb. station: — ? — ; habitat: St. Thomas; de Candé! remark: Described by d'Orb. in „moll. de Cuba" 1—227 pl. 17 fig. 7—9.

T. **laevis** Ad. station: — ? — ; habitat: Jamaica; Ad.! St. Thomas; Krebs!

T. **latior** Ad. station: — ? — ; habitat: Jamaica; Ad.! St. Thomas; Krebs!

T. **modesta** d'Orb. station: — ? — ; habitat: Jamaica; Candé! remark: Described by d'Orb. „moll. de Cuba" 1—222 pl. 16 fig. 22. 24.

T. **multicostata** Ad. station: — ? — ; habitat: Jamaica; Ad.!

T. **obeliscus** Ad. station: — ? — ; habitat: Jamaica; Ad.!

T. **ornata** d'Orb. station: — ? — ; habitat: Martinique; Guadeloupe; Jamaica; Candé! Jamaica; Ad.! Guadeloupe; Beau! remark: Described in d'Orb. „moll. de Cuba“ 1—221 pl. 16 fig. 18. 21.

T. pulchella d'Orb. station: — ? —; habitat: Martinique; St. Thomas; Guadeloupe; Candé! Cuba; Sagra! Guadeloupe; Beau! remark: Described by d'Orbig. in „Moll. de Cuba“ 1. 220 pl. 16 fig. 14—17.

T. punctata Ad. station: — ? —; habitat: Jamaica; Ad.!

T. pupoides d'Orb. station: — ? —; habitat: Cuba; St. Thomas; d'Orb.! Guadeloupe; Beau! remark: Described by d'Orb. in „Moll. de Cuba“ 1. 224. pl. 16. fig. 32. 36.

T. pusilla Ad. station: — ? — ; habitat: Jamaica; Ad.! St. Thomas; Krebs!

T. reticulata Ad. station: — ? — ; habitat: Jamaica; Ad.! St. Thomas; Krebs!

T. simplex d'Orb. station: — ? — ; habitat: Jamaica; Candé! remark: Described by d'Orb. in „Moll. de Cuba“ 1—224 pl. 16. 28—31.

T. substriata Ad. station: — ? — ; habitat: Jamaica; Ad.! St. Thomas; Krebs!

T. subulata Ad. station: — ? —; habitat: Jamaica; Ad.! St. Thomas; Knox!

T. turris d'Orb. station: — ? — ; habitat: St. Thomas; d'Orb.! R. Swift! remark: Described by d'Orb. in „moll. de Cuba“ 1—219. pl. 16. fig. 10—13.

Eulimacea.

Eulima Risso.

E. affinis Ad. station: — ? —; habitat: Jamaica; Ad.!

E. arcuata Ad. station: — ? — ; habitat: Jamaica; Ad.!

E. bifasciata d'Orb. station: — ? —; habitat: Guadeloupe; St. Thomas; de Candé! Guadeloupe; Beau! St. Thomas; R. Swift! remark: Described in „Moll. de Cuba" 1. 216. pl. 16 fig. 1—3; is this not E. fulvo cincta Ad.?

E. conica Ad. station: — ? —; habitat: Jamaica; Ad.!

E. fulvo-cincta Ad. station: — ? —; habitat: Jamaica; Ad.! St. Thomas; Knox!

E. gracilis Ad. station: — ? —; habitat: Jamaica; Ad.!

E. incerta d'Orb. station: — ? —; habitat: Jamaica; de Candé! remark: Described in „Moll. de Cuba" 1—218 pl. 16 fig. 7—9.

E. jamaicensis Ad. station: — ? —; habitat: Jamaica; St. Thomas; St. Johns; Ad.! St. Martin; St. Barth; St. Thomas; St. Johns; Krebs!

E. subcarinata d'Orb. station: — ? —; habitat: Guadeloupe; de Candé! Beau! remark: Described in „Moll. de Cuba" 1—217 pl. 16 fig. 4—6.

Vermetacea.

Vermetus Adanson.

V. corrodeus d'Orb. station: on rocks close to the surface of the sea; habitat :Cuba; Martinique; d'Orb.!

V. decussata Gml. station: — ? —; habitat: West-Indies; Mörch pg. 53.

V. irrigularis d'Orb. station: — ? —; habitat: Cuba; Martinique; de Candé!

V. lumbricalis L. (V. Knorii D.) station: on rocks in the surface of the sea; habitat: Cuba; Auber! St. Thomas; Krebs!

Siliquaria Brugiére.

S. muricata Born. (S. echinata Gml.) station: found on sandy beaches; habitat: West-Indies; Mörch pg. 53!

1 spec. ind. station: between small shells picked on the beach; habitat: Porto-Plata; Krebs!

Caecacea.

Caecum Fleming. 3 spec. ind.: St. Thomas; Krebs!

Siphonariacea.

Siphonaria Sowerby.

S. lineata d'Orb. station: — ? —; habitat: Cuba; Sagra! Guadeloupe; Beau!

S. picta d'Orb. station: — ? —; habitat: Cuba; Auber! Rio Janeiro; d'Orb.!

Acmaeacea.

Acmaea Eschholtz.

A. fungus Meush. (P. fungoides Bolt., P. octoradiata var. Gm.) station: — ? —; habitat: West-Indies; Mörch!

A. Hamillei Fisch. station: — ? —; habitat: Guadeloupe; Beau!

A. leucopleura Gm. (C. extinctorium? Sowb. C. rugosa Less) station: — ? —; habitat: West-Indies; Mörch! Cuba; St. Lucy; Martinique; d'Orb.! Jamaica; St. Thomas; Ad.!

A. melaleuca Gm. station: — ? —; habitat: West-Indies; Mörch!

A. melanosticta Gm. (L. antillarum Sow. Pat. palescens Ph.) station: — ? —; habitat: West-Indies; Mörch! St. Thomas; Krebs!

A. pustula Helb. (P. punctulata Gm., P. puncturata . . .)

station: on flat pieces of Madrepores close to the shore;
habitat: West-Indies; Mörch pg. 144! Turks-Island;
St. Johns; Jamaica; St. Thomas; Ad.! Guadeloupe; Beau!
Barbadoes; Trinidad; St. Martin; Anguilla; St. Barth;
St. Johns; St. Thomas; St. Croix; Puertoricco; Porto-
Plata; Krebs!

Neritacea.

Nerita Linné.

N. antillarum Gm. station: — ? —; habitat: West-
Indies; d'Orb.! St. Thomas? Carthagena? St. Martha?
Krebs! remark: Yellow columella, one tooth, spire flat;
we are in doubt if those we have found, at the three
places noted, are N. ant. Gm.

N. nigerrima Chem. station: on wood along the shore
in creeks with smooth water; habitat: West-Indies;
Mörch pg. 168! Porto-Plata? Krebs!

N. peloronta L. (Pila Kl. N. erythrodon. Recluz.) station: On rocks from 1 foot below low water and until
2 to 3 feet above highwater; habitat: West-Indies;
Mörch pg. 169! Jamaica; Havana; Bermuda; Carthagena; Ad.! St. Thomas; St. Johns; Guadeloupe; Barbadoes; St. Martin; Carthagena; Krebs! Cuba; Sagra!
Auber! Candé! Martinique; d'Orb.!

N. praecognita C. B. Ad.! station: On rocks from 1
foot below low-water until 2 to 3 feet above highwater;
habitat: Jamaica; Ad.! Guadeloupe; Beau! St. Thomas; St. Johns; St. Croix; Carthagena; Krebs! remark:
A doubtful species.

N. varia Meuschen. (Theliostyla Mörch, N. tesselata Gml.)
station: On rocks where the waves washe over; West-
Indies; Mörch pg. 168! Cuba; Sagra! Auber! Martini-

que; Candé! Guadeloupe; Beau! St. Thomas; St. Johns;
Sta. Martha; Carthagena; Krebs!

N. variegata Chem. (N. versicolor Gml., Neritina striata
Chem. acc. to d'Orb.) station: On rocks where the waves
wash over; habitat: Cuba; Martinique; d'Orb.! Florida; Alphen! Ad.! West-Indies; Mörch pg. 169! Guadeloupe; Beau! Duchassain! St. Thomas; St. Johns;
Porto-Plata; Carthagena; Krebs! Turks-Island; Havana;
Jamaica; Arecibo; Carthagena; Ad.!

Neretina Lamarck.

N. brasiliana Recluz. (N. virginea Lmk. acc. to Beau.)
station: — ? — ; habitat: Guadeloupe; Beau!

N. chlorina Link. (N. meleagris Lmk.) station: In sea
water in small ponds in the rocks along the shore and
on poles where the sea is calm and smooth; habitat:
West-Indies; Mörch pg. 167! Cuba; Guadeloupe; d'Orb.!
Guadeloupe; Beau! St. Domingo; Lmk.! Jamaica; Carthagena; Ad.! St. Thomas; Carthagena; Krebs!

N. Domingensis Lmk. station: — ? — ; habitat:
St. Domingo; Lmk.!

N. jamaicensis Ad. station: — ? — ; habitat: Jamaica; E. Chitty!

N. microstoma d'Orb. station: — ? — ; habitat:
Martinique; de Candé!

N. ornata Ad. station: — ? — ; habitat: Jamaica; Ad!

N. pulchella Gray. station: — ? — ; West-Indies;
Mörch pg. 167!

N. punctulata Lmk. (N. cassicula Sow. acc. to Beau!
N. fluviatilis? acc. to C. B. Adams) station: — ? — ;
habitat: Martinique; Mörch! Guadeloupe; Beau! Du-
chassing! d'Orb.! Jamaica! Ad.!

N. pupa L. station: In brackish water even a good distance from the sea; habitat: Guadeloupe; Beau! Duchassain! Cuba; Sagra! Auber! West-Indies; Mörch pg. 167! St. Croix; A. H. Riise! Arecibo; Jamaica; Ad.! Porto-Plata; Krebs!

N. pusilla Ad. station: — ? — ; habitat: Jamaica; Adams!

N. pygmæa Ad. station: — ? — ; habitat: Jamaica; Ad.!

N. succinea Recluz. station: — ? — ; habitat: Guadeloupe; Beau! Crabisland; A. H. Riise! St. Thomas; H. Haagensen! St. Johns (Fishbay); Krebs!

N. tenebrosa Ad. (N. fluviatilis? according to C. B. Ad.) station: — ? — ; habitat: Jamaica; Ad.!

N. trabalis Meusch. station: — ? — ; habitat: West-Indies; Mörch pg. 167!

N. tristis d'Orb. (syn. N. pupa L. accord. to Jay's Catal.) station: — ? — ; habitat: Guadeloupe; Beau! Cuba; Sagra! Jamaica; Ad.! St. Croix; A. H. Riise!

N. turriculata Mke. (N. virginea Sow.) station: — ? — ; West-Indies; Mörch pg. 166!

N. virginea L. station: In brackish water, sometime in a considerable distance from the shore (at North-Star. St. Croix) in salt water in the wester-most part of the harbour of St. Thomas; habitat: West-Indies; Mörch pg. 166! Florida; d'Orbig.! Cuba; Sagra! Auber! Martinique; Guadeloupe; Candé! Hotessier! Jamaica; St. Domingo; Arecibo; Ad.! St. Thomas; St. Croix; Krebs!

N. viridis L. station: In salt and brackish water; on poles in the western part of the harbour of St. Thomas, where the sea is smooth; habitat: West-Indies; Mörch! Martinique; St. Lucy; Guadeloupe; Candé! Cuba; d'Orb.!

Guadeloupe; Beau! Jamaica; St. Johns; Arecibo; Bermuda; Ad.! St. Thomas; St. Croix; St. Johns; St. Barth; Anguilla; St. Martin; Trinidad; Porto-Plata; Krebs!

Trochacea.

Phasianella Lamarck.

P. affinis Ad. station: Below Madrepores in 1 or 2 feet water; habitat: St. Thomas; St. Johns; Jamaica; Ad.! St. Thomas; St. Barth; Krebs!

P. brevis Ad. station: — ? — ; habitat: Jamaica; St. Thomas; Ad.!

P. brevis d'Orb. station: — ? — ; habitat: Cuba; Sagra! Martinique; Candé! remark: Described in „moll. de Cuba" 2—79 pl. 20 fig. 19—21.

P. concinna Ad. station: — ? — ; Jamaica; Ad.! St. Thomas; St. Martin; St. Barth; Krebs! St. Thomas; Crab-island; Coro; A. H. Riise!

P. concolor Ad. station: — ? — ; habitat: Jamaica; Ad.!

P. tesselata Ad. (P. minuta Ant., P. lipeata Dkr. according to specimens in the collection of A. H. Riise) station: — ? — ; habitat: Jamaica; Ad.! Guadeloupe; Beau! Hotessier! St. Johns; Anguilla; Trinidad; Krebs!

P. umbilicata d'Orb. station: dredged May 1860 from 10 to 12 fathoms water, bluish sandy mud, 2 specimens; habitat: Martinique; Guadeloupe; Jamaica; Cuba; Candé! Sagra! Guadeloupe; Beau! St. Thomas; Krebs! remark: Described in „moll. de Cuba" 2—78 pl. 19 fig. 35—37.

Turbo Linné.

T. Cailletii Fischer & Bern. station: Taken in a fish; habitat: Guadeloupe; Beau!

T. castaneus Chem. (T. hippocastanum Lmk.) station: Between Zostera (maritima?) on 2 to 3 feet water in the western part of the harbour of St. Thomas; habitat: West-Indies; Mörch pg. 162! Margarita; R. Swift! St. Thomas; Tortola; St. Martin; Guadeloupe; Trinidad; Porto - Plata; Krebs! Martinique; Jamaica; Cuba; Florida; d'Orb.!

T. crenulatus Chem. station: — ? — ; habitat: West-Indies; Mörch pg. 162! Guadeloupe; Beau!

T. pica L. station: on rocks where the waves are washing over; habitat: West-Indies; Mörch pg. 154! Guadeloupe; Beau! Cuba; Martinique; Guadeloupe; Sagra! Auber! Candé! Jamaica; Carthagena; Ad.! St. Thomas; Bermuda; St. Croix; St. Johns; Porto - Plata; Krebs! remark: common food between the lower classes.

Lictia Gray.

L. cruentata Mühlf. (Delphinula radiata Kien.) station: Under pieces of Madrepores in 2 to 3 feet water, where the sea is pretty rough; habitat: West-Indies; Mörch! Guadeloupe; Beau! Duchassain! Jamaica; Ad.! St. Thomas; Anguilla; Krebs!

Delphinula Lamk.

D. tuberculosa d'Orb. (Trochus Schrammii Fischer accor. to Beau) station: — ? — ; habitat: Jamaica; St. Thomas; Candé! Guadeloupe; Beau! remark: Described in „moll. de Cuba" 2—66.

Vitrinella Adams (Skoenia acc. to Beau).

V. Adamsii Fischer. station: found dead in the fine white sand of the beach; habitat: Guadeloupe; Beau!

V. **Beauii** Fischer. station: — ? — ; habitat: Guadeloupe; Beau!

V. **helicoidea** Ad. station: in the fine white sand of the beach; habitat: Jamaica; Ad.! St. Thomas; Krebs!

V. **hyalina** Ad. station: — ? — ; habitat: Jamaica; Ad.!

V. **interrupta** Ad. station: — ? — ; habitat: Jamaica; Ad.!

V. **megastoma** Ad. station: — ? — ; habitat: Jamaica; Ad.! Guadeloupe; Beau!

V. **Petitii** Fisch. station: — ? — ; |habitat: Guadeloupe; Beau!

V. **Schrammii** Fisch. station: — ? —; habitat: Jamaica; Ad.!

V. **tincta** Ad. station: —?—; habitat: Jamaica; Ad.!

Calcar D. Montfort (Stella Kl.)

C. **caelatus** Chem. station: on coarse gravel in 4 to 5 feet water; habitat: West-Indies; Mörch pg. 160! Cuba; Sagra! Auber! Martinique; Guadeloupe; St. Lucy; Candé! Guadeloupe; Beau! Bermuda; St. Johns; St. Thomas; Jamaica; Ad.! St. Thomas; Tortola; Krebs!

C. **inermis** Gml. station: — ? — ; habitat: Cuba; Sagra! Martinique; St. Croix; Candé! St. Thomas; Kr.! remark: This is certainly nothing else than the young Calcar Tuber L.; we have compared it with the drawing of Chemnitz.

C. **ramosus** Meusch. (T. imbricatus Gml.) station: — ? — ; habitat: West-Indies; Mörch pg. 160! Curaçao; A. H. Riise! St. Thomas; St. Croix; Tortola; Guadeloupe; Kr.!

C. **Spenglerianus** Ch. (Tuber aculeatus Gml.) station:

Said to live in very deep water; habitat: Ind. orient;
Mörch pg. 160! Curaçao; R. Swift! Guadeloupe; Beau!
Jamaica; Ad.! Porto - Plata; St. Martin; Krebs! re-
mark: perfect specimens are very rare.

C. Tuber L. station: On rocks near the shore in 1 to
8 feet water; habitat: West-Indies; Mörch pg. 160!
Guadeloupe; Beau! Jamaica; Arecibo; Bermuda; Ad.!
Trinidad; St. Martin; St. Johns; Kr.!

Astralium Link. (Imperator Mtf.).

A. brevispinum Lmk. station: — ? — ; habitat: Cuba;
Martinique; Candé!

A. calcar L. (T. inermis Gml.? T. spinulosa Lmk. Ki.?)
station: — ? — ; habitat: West-Indies; Mörch pag.
160! Cuba; Sagra! Martinique; Candé! Guadeloupe;
Beau! remark: see A. phoebia Bolt. & Calcar inermis Gml.

A. costulatum (Tr.) Lmk. station: — ? — ; habitat:
West-Indies; Lamarck! St. Croix; Kr.!

A. phoebia Bolt. (A. deplanatum Link. P. longispina Lmk.)
station: In Marsch 58, found on sand about ½ foot
below the level of the sea; habitat: West-Indies; Mörch
pg. 160! St. Thomas; Candé! Guadeloupe; Beau! St.
Thomas; St. Croix; Tortola; Carthagena; Kr.! remark:
We have no doubt that the A. calcar L. and A. phoebia B. are synonymes; 1721—22 in Chemnitz are certainly young specimens of A. ph.

A. radians Lmk. station: — ? — ; habitat: Near
Guadeloupe; Lmk.! St. Croix; Krebs!

A. rhodostomum Lmk. station: on a rock about the
level of the sea. June 52; habitat: St. Martha-New-
Granada; Kr.! remark: those found at St. Martha

are the only specimens seen by the collectors at St. Thomas.

Globulus Schum. (Rotella Lmk. d'Orb.)

G. anomalis d'Orb. station: — ? — ; habitat: St. Thomas; Candé! remark: Described in „Moll. de Cuba" 2—64.

G. carinatus d'Orb. station: — ? — ; habitat: St. Thomas; Candé! remark: Described in „moll. de Cuba" 2—62.

G. diaphanus d'Orb. station: — ? — ; habitat: St. Thomas; Candé! remark: Described in „moll. de Cuba" 2—62.

G. semistriatus d'Orb. station: — ? — ; habitat: Cuba; Sagra! remark: Described in „moll. de Cuba" 2—61.

G. strictus d'Orb. station: — ? —; habitat: Jamaica Candé!

Trochus Linné.

T. asperulus Lamarck station: — ? — habitat: St. Domingo; Lmk.!

T. aster Ph. station: — ? — ; habitat: Guadeloupe; Beau!

T. ater Less. station: — ? —; habitat: West-Indies; Mörch pg. 154!

T. concavus Gml. station: — ? — ; habitat: Martinique; d'Orb.!

T. crenulatus Wood. station: — ? — ; habitat: St. Johns; St. Thomas; Jamaica; Ad.! Carthagena; Kr.!

T. cubanus Ph. station: — ? — ; habitat: Guadeloupe; Beau!

T. excavatus Lmk. (Tr. umbilicaris Ch.) station: On rocks near the shore at the level of the sea; habitat: West-Indies; Mörch pg. 153! Martinique; Guadeloupe; Cande! Hotessier! Guadeloupe; Beau! Jamaica; Ad.! St. Thomas; St. Croix; St. Johns; Crabisland; Porto-Plata; Krebs!

T. fasciatus Born. (C. lun. laevis Chem., Tb. dentatus Gm., Tb. carneolus Lmk., Tr. livido-maculatus Ad.) station: Under pieces of Madrepores in 1 foot water; habitat: Jamaica; Ad.! West-Indies; Mörch! Martinique; Guadeloupe; St. Lucy; Hotessier! Candé! Cuba; Sagra! St. Thomas; St. Johns; St. Martin; Anguilla; Trinidad; Barbadoes; Porto-Plata; Krebs! Guadeloupe; Beau!

T. flammulatus Lmk. station: — ? — ; habitat: St. Domingo; Lmk.

T. heliacus Ph. station: — ? — ; habitat: Guadeloupe; Beau!

T. Hotessierianus d'Orb. (Tr. occultus Phil., Tr. nassaviensis Ch., Tr. interrupta striatus C. B. Ad.) station: In small ponds of seawater in the rocks, left when it is low-water; habitat: West-Indies; Mörch pg. 153! Florida; d'Orb.! Guadeloupe; St. Lucy; Candé! Hotessier! Cuba; Auber; Sagra! St. Thomas; St. Martin; Porto-Plata; Kr.! Guadeloupe; Beau!

T. javanicus Lmk. station: Said to be taken on corals in 3 fathoms water; habitat: Jamaica; Ad.! Carupano; Kr.!

T. indusii Chem. (Omphalius Ph., Tr. carneus Gml., Tr. canaliculatus d'Orb., Tr. scalaris Anton, Tr. crenulatus Bolt.); station: On pieces of madrepores in 1 or 2 feet of water; habitat: West-Indies; Mörch pg. 153! Cuba; Auber! All the Virgin-Islands; Krebs!

T. jujubinus Gml. (Tr. lunatus Bolt.) station: On pieces of Madrepores in 2 feet water; habitat: West-Indies; Mörch pg. 157! Jamaica; St. Thomas; Carthagena; Ad.! All the Virgin Islands; Kr.!

T. microstomus d'Orb. (Tr. bidentatus Mk.) station: — ? — ; habitat: West-Indies; Mörch pg. 154!

T. pulcher C. B. Adams. station: On pieces of madrepores in a few feet water and dredged from 6 and from 12 feet water on bluish sandy mud; habitat: Jamaica; Ad.! St. Thomas; St. Croix; Porto-Plata; Krebs! remark: Described in C. B. Adams „Contributions" page 69— ; should this species not be Woods Tr. interruptus? We have specimens of pulcher with 9 whorls.

T. Schrammii Fisch. see Delph. tuberculosa d'Orb.

Stomatia Helbling.

S. picta d'Orb. station: On pieces of Madrepores in a few feet water; habitat: Cuba; d'Orbig.! St. Martin; Guadeloupe; Beau! St. Thomas; St. Barth; Pto.-Plata; Anguilla; Krebs! remark: Described in „Moll. de Cuba" 2—184 pl. 24 fig. 19, 21.

Stomatella Lamarck.

S. coccinea A. Ad. station: — ? — ; habitat: St. Thomas; Mörch pg. 152! St. Thomas; St. Croix; Kr.!

Pleurotomaria Defrance.

P. Gouayana Fisch. & Bern. station: In very deep water; habitat: Marie Galante; Beau!

Fissurellacea.

Emarginula Lamarck.

1. Emarginula.

E. notata L. (P. manipula Humphr) station: — ? — ; habitat: West-Indies; Mörch pg. 148!

E. Rollandii Fisch. station: — ? —; habitat: Guadeloupe; Beau!

2. Subemarginula.

E. depressa Blainw. station: — ? —; habitat: Guadeloupe; Beau! remark: C. B. Adams gave us a specimen of E. octoradiata Gml. from St. Thomas with this name.

E. octoradiata Gml. (E. tricarinata Sow., P. laqueara Gray, E. Listeri Ant.) station: Common on rocks between high and low-water mark; habitat: West-Indies; Mörch pg. 149! Jamaica; St. Johns; Ad.! St. Thomas; St. Johns; St. Barth; St. Martin; Anguilla; Barbadoes; Porto-Plata; Kr.!

Fissurella Bruguiére.

F. alternata Say. station: — ? —; habitat: Guadeloupe; Beau! Jamaica; Carthagena; Ad.!

F. Antillarum d'Orb. station: — ? —; habitat: Florida; Cuba; d'Orb.! remark: Described in „moll. de Cuba" 2—198 pl. 24 fig. 40—42.

F. atricapilla Dw. (F. viridula Lmk.) station: — ? —; habitat: West-Indies; Mörch pg. 149!

F. barbadensis Gml. (P. porphyrozonias Gml., P. angusta Gml., F. radiata Lmk.) station: On rocks from high-water-mark until 4 to 5 feet below the level of the sea; habitat: Florida; Cuba; St. Lucy; Martinique; d'Orb.! West-Indies; Mörch pg. 149! Jamaica; Ad.! Guadeloupe; Beau! St. Thomas; St. Croix; Crabisland; St. Johns; St. Martin; Anguilla; Puertoricco; Pto.-Plata; Kr.!

F. cancellata Sal. (F. Sowerbyi Guild.) station: — ? —; habitat: Guadeloupe; Beau! St. Thomas; St. Martin; St. Barth; Kr.!

F. sayennensis Lmk. station: — ? — ; habitat: Guadeloupe; Beau!

F. Dysonii Reeve. station: — ? — ; habitat: St. Johns; Ad.! Guadeloupe; Beau!

F. elongata Reeve. station: — ? — ; habitat: Guadeloupe; Beau! St. Thomas; St. Martin; St. Barth; Kr.!

F. fascicularis Lmk. (Clypidella Sow.) station: — ? — ; habitat: Jamaica; Ad.! Arecibo; Newton! West-Indies; Mörch pg. 150!

F. gemmulata Reeve. (F. minuta Sowb., F. elongata Ad.) station: On pieces of Madrepores in a few feet water; habitat: Guadeloupe; Beau! Jamaica; Ad.! St. Thomas; St. Johns; St. Croix; Crabisland; St. Barth; St. Martin; Anguilla; Kr.! remark: We have in a note by C. B. Adams seen that he considered F. gemmulata Reeve synonyme with F. elongata Ad.

F. graeca L. (F. Listeri d'Orb.) station: — ? — ; habitat: West-Indies; Mörch pg. 149! St. Thomas; St. Johns; St. Martin; Porto-Plata; Kr.! St. Lucy; Martinique; d'Orb.! St. Thomas; St. Johns; Jamaica; Arecibo; Carthagena; Ad.! remark: Moll. de Cuba 2—197 pl. 24 fig. 37—39.

F. larva Reeve. station: — ? — ; habitat: Guadeloupe; Beau! St. Martin; Guadeloupe; Kr.! St. Johns; Adams!

F. nimbosa Lmk. station: At Carthagena on rocks where the waves broke over; habitat: Martinique; Candé! Guadeloupe; Beau! Carthagena, Kr.!

F. nodosa Born. (F. spinosa Gml. acc. to Mörch, F. jamaicensis Gml. acc. to C. B. Ad.) station: On rocks from highwater mark to 3 to 6 feet under the level of the sea, especielly between seaweed; habitat: West-

Indies; Mörch pg. 149! Jamaica; Arecibo; Ad.! Cuba;
St. Lucy; Martinique; d'Orb.! Guadeloupe; Beau! St.
Thomas; St. Croix; Puertoricco; Pto.-Plata; Kr.!

F. pustula L. station: — ? —; habitat: West-Indies;
Mörch pg. 150! Cuba; Florida; d'Orb.! Guadeloupe;
Beau! St. Thomas; St. Croix; St. Martin; Crabisland;
Anguilla; Puertoricco; Pto.-Plata; Kr.! Guadeloupe; St.
Johns; Ad.!

F. radiata Lmk. (F. balanoides? Reeve acc. to Beau) station: — ? —; habitat: Guadeloupe; Beau!

F. reticulata Say. station: — ? — ; habitat: Jamaica; Ad.!

F. rosea Lmk. station: — ? — ; habitat: Jamaica;
Arecibo; Ad.! remark: „Compare it with F. barbadensis" says C. B. Adams in a note.

F. viridula Lmk. station: — ? — ; habitat: Guadeloupe; Beau! St. Thomas; Jamaica; Arecibo; Ad.!

Patellacea.

Patella Linné.

P. albicosta C. B. Ad. station: — ? — ; habitat:
Jamaica; Ad.! Guadeloupe; Beau!

P. confusa Guild. (P. notata Lmk.) station: — ? — ;
habitat: Guadeloupe; Beau!

P. cubaniana d'Orb. station: — ? — ; habitat:
Cuba; Florida; d'Orb.!

P. cubensis Reeve. station: — ? — ; habitat: Guadeloupe; Beau!

P. elegans Ph. station: — ? — ; habitat: St. Thomas; Kr.!

P. notata Chem. station: — ? —; habitat: St. Thomas; Jamaica; Arecibo; Ad.!

P. pulcherrima Guild. (P. Candeana d'Orb.) station: — ? —; habitat: Guadeloupe; Beau! Cuba; St. Lucy; Martinique; Guadeloupe; d'Orb.!

Chitonacea.

Chiton Linné.

C. acutiliratus Reeve. (Ch. pectinatus Sow. acc. to Beau) station: — ? — ; habitat: West-Indies; Mörch pg. 139! Guadeloupe; Beau!

C. asper Schut. station: — ? — ; habitat: Guadeloupe; Beau!

C. assimilis Reeve. station: On rocks near the surface of the sea; habitat: Guadeloupe; Beau! St. Thomas; Krebs!

C. candisatus Shut. station: — ? —; habitat: Guadeloupe; Beau!

C. costatus Ad. station: — ? — ; habitat: Jamaica; Ad.!

C. Erythronatus C. B. Ad. station: — ? — ; habitat: Jamaica; Ad.! Guadeloupe; Beau!

C. granulatus Gml. station: — ? —; habitat: Cuba; Martinique; d'Orb.!

C. marmoratus Ch. (Lophorus Poli, C. marmoreus Ch., C. punctatus L.?) station: On rocks along the shores; habitat: Barbadoes; Mörch pg. 138! Guadeloupe; Beau! Jamaica; Arecibo; Ad.! St. Croix; Carthagena; Kr.!

C. marmoratus Reeve. station: — ? -- ; habitat: Guadeloupe; Beau!

C. multicostatus Ad. station: — ? — ; habitat: Jamaica; Ad.!

C. papillosus Ad. station: — ? — ; habitat: Jamaica; Ad.! Guadeloupe; Beau!

C. **piceus** Gml. station: On rocks at the surface of the sea at St. Thomas; Carthagena June 52; Bermuda 25 April 1858; habitat: West-Indies; Mörch pg. 139! Guadeloupe; Beau! St. Johns; Jamaica; Bermuda; Ad.! Carthagena; Bermuda; St. Thomas; Kr.! St. Thomas; R. Swift!

C. **purpurascens** Ad. station: — ? — ; habitat: Jamaica; Ad.! Guadeloupe; Beau!

C. **rugosus** Gray. (C. sqvalidus Ad. acc. to Ad.) station: — ? — ; habitat: Jamaica; Ad.!

C. **salamandra** Spl (C. piceus var. Gml., C. occidentalis Reeve acc. to Mörch, C. marmoreus Reeve syn. with C. occidentalis Reeve acc. to Beau) station: On rocks at the shore of Carthagena; habitat: West-Indies; Mörch pg. 139! Carthagena; Kr.!

C. **Schrammii** Shut. station: — ? — ; habitat: Guadeloupe; Beau!

C. **spiculosus** Gray. station: — ? — ; habitat: Guadeloupe; Beau!

C. **squamosus** L. (C. scaber variegatus Ch., Scutigerulus angulatus Meusch., C. marmoreus Reeve) station: on rocks close to the shore; habitat: West-Indies; Mörch pg. 138! Guadeloupe; Beau! St. Thomas; R. Swift! Jamaica; Porto-Cabello; Ad.! Carthagena; Kr.!

C. **squamulosus** C. B. Ad. station: — ? — ; habitat: Guadeloupe; Beau! Jamaica; Ad.!

C. **strigatus** (Chitonella) Shutt. (C. laevis Reeve. acc. to Beau) station: — ? — ; habitat: Guadeloupe; Beau!

C. **undatus** Spgl. (C. squamosus Born, Ch., Lmk., C. tuberculatus L.?) station: — ? — ; habitat: West-Indies; Mörch pg. 138!

C. **viridis** Spgl., Wood (C. squamosus denticulatus Ch.,

C. foveolatus Sowb. accord. to Mörch, C. excavatus
Gray acc. to Beau) s t a t i o n : — ? —; h a b i t a t : Guadeloupe; Beau! West-Indies; Mörch pg. 138!

Dentalium Linné.

D. a n t i l l a r u m d'Orb. s t a t i o n : — ? —; h a b i t a t : St.
Thomas; d'Orb.! Guadeloupe; Beau!

D. d i s p a r i l e d'Orb. s t a t i o n : — ? —; h a b i t a t : Martinique; d'Orb.! Guadeloupe; Beau!

D. d o m i n g e n s e d'Orb. s t a t i o n : — ? —; h a b i t a t :
St. Domingo; Martinique; St. Thomas; Cuba; d'Orb.!

D. s e m i s t r i a t u m Guild. s t a t i o n : — ? — ; h a b i t a t :
Guadeloupe; Beau!

Aplysiacea.
Aplysia Linné.

A. p r o t e a Rang. s t a t i o n : feeds on species of Ulvae, close
to the shore in smooth water; h a b i t a t : Guadeloupe;
Beau! St. Thomas; Carthagena; Kr.! r e m a r k : we have
observed it swiming but not as George Johnston says in
Einl. in die Conchyphiologie. Stuttgard 1853 pag. 127
„with the foot upward“, but with the matel extended as
mentioned pg. 129; it swims quick when alarmed and
takes then a shape very different from when it crawls
about.

Lophocercus Krohn.

1 species i n d. at St. Thomas; Krebs!

Lobiger Krohn.

L. S o w e r b i i Fischer. s t a t i o n : — ? —; h a b i t a t : Guadeloupe; Beau!

Bullacea.

Aplustrum Schumacher.

A. physis L. & d'Orb. (Hydalina filosa Sch.) station
—? —; habitat: West-Indies; Mörch pg. 136! Cuba;
St. Lucy; d'Orb.! Guadeloupe; Hotessier! Beau! St. Thomas; Krebs!

Bullinula Beck.

B. undata Brug. (B. nitidula Sol., B. elegans Mke.) station: —? —; habitat: West-Indies; Mörch pg. 136!
Cuba; Sagra! St. Vincent; Guilding! St. Johns; Ad.!
Guadeloupe; Beau! St. Thomas; St. Croix; St. Martin; Kr.!

Bulla Linné.

B. acuta d'Orb. station: — ? — ; habitat: Cuba;
Sagra! Jamaica; St. Thomas; Guadeloupe; Martinique;
Candé! Guadeloupe; Beau!

B. antillarum d'Orb. station: — ? — ; habitat: St.
Thomas; d'Orb.! Guadeloupe; Beau!

B. Auberii d'Orb. station: — ? — ; habitat: Cuba;
d'Orbig.!

B. bidentata d'Orb. station: — ? — ; habitat: Cuba;
Sagra! Jamaica; St. Thomas; Guadeloupe; Martinique;
d'Orb.! Guadeloupe; Beau! Porto-Plata; St. Thomas;
Krebs!

B. canaliculata d'Orb. (see Actaeon) station: — ? —;
habitat: Cuba; Sagra! St. Thomas; Porto-Plata; Kr.!

B. Candeana d'Orb. (see Philine) station: — ? —;
habitat: Cuba; Sagra! Guadeloupe; Beau! Guadeloupe;
Martinique; St. Thomas; Jamaica; Candé!

B. caribaea d'Orb. station: May 60, 3 specimens in

10 to 12 fathoms water on bluish sandy mud; habitat: Jamaica; St. Thomas; Martinique; Guadeloupe; Candé! Cuba; d'Orb.! Guadeloupe; Beau! Porto-Plata; Krebs! remark: 1 specimen is double the size as the shell described by d'Orb.

B. fragilis Lmk. station: — ? — ; habitat: Guadeloupe; Beau!

B. maculosa Mart. (B. ibyx Meusch., B. umbilicata Bolt., B. striata Brug. non Ph., B. media Ph.) station: — ? — ; habitat: West-Indies; Mörch pg. 136! Guadeloupe; Beau! Jamaica; Arecibo; Turksisland; Ad.! St. Thomas; St. Croix; St. Johns; Tortola; St. Martin; St. Barth; Barbadoes; Trinidad; Krebs!

B. Petitii d'Orb. station: on bluish mud in 10—12 fathoms water; May 1860 dredged 4 dead and 3 life specimens; habitat: Cuba; Auber! St. Thomas; Krebs! remark: the animal greenish and according to the three strong canaliculated semilunar teeth an Atys.

B. recta d'Orb. station: — ? — ; habitat: St. Thomas; Guadeloupe; Candé! Guadeloupe; Beau! Jamaica; Ad.! St. Thomas; Krebs!

B. physis Linné. station: — ? —; habitat: St. Thomas; Krebs!

B. Sagrae d'Orb. station: — ? —; habitat: Martinique; Candé!

B. solida Gml. (B. ampulla d'Orb.) station: — ? — ; habitat: West-Indies; Mörch pg. 136! Cuba; Sagra! Guadeloupe; Hotessier! Martinique; de Candé!

B. sulcata d'Orb. station: — ? —; habitat: St. Thomas; Candé! Guadeloupe; Candé! Beau! Porto-Plata; Krebs!

B. undata Brug. is a Bullinula.

Atys de Montfort.

A. Guildingii Sow. station: — ? —; habitat: West-
Indies; Mörch pg. 135! Jamaica; Ad.! St. Thomas; St.
Martin; Kr.!

Philine Ascanias (Bullaea Lmk.).

P. candeana (Bullaea) d'Orb. station: — ? — ; habitat: Guadeloupe; Candé! Beau!

Actaeon de Montfort (Tornatella).

A. canaliculata (Bulla) d'Orb. (B. olivula C. B. Ad.,
T. bullata Ki.?) station: — ? — ; habitat: Guadeloupe; Beau! West-Indies; Mörch pg. 136!

Dimyaria.
1. Tellinacea.
Venus Linné.

V. affinis Gm. (C. laeta Lmk. non Linné) station: — ?
— ; habitat: Antillae; Mörch pg. 27!

V. albida Gm. (Cyth. albida Gray acc. to C. B. Adams)
station: — ? — ; habitat: Carthagena (from Krebs!);
St. Thomas; Jamaica; C. B. Ad.!

V. antillarum d'Orb. station: — ? — ; habitat: Florida; Cuba; St. Thomas; Jamaica; Martinique; d'Orb.!
remark: Moll. de Cuba 2—278 pl. 26 fig. 41—43.

V. Auberiana d'Orb. station: — ? — ; habitat:
Cuba; Auber! St. Thomas; R. Swift! remark: Moll.
de Cuba 2—227 pl. 26 fig. 35, 37.

V. Beauii Recl. (see V. subrostrata Lmk.) station: — ?
— ; habitat: Guadeloupe; Beau! (p. 24).

V. cardioides Lmk. station: — ? — ; habitat:
Cayenne; Jamaica; Lmk.!

V. circinata Born. (Dione; Cyth. guineensis Lmk.) station: in white fine sand on 2 to 4 feet water in creeks
where the water is smooth; habitat: Brasilia; Mörch
pg. 27! Guadeloupe; Beau pg. 24! Jamaica; Ad.! Virgin-Island; R. Swift!*) St. Thomas; Trinidad; Carthagena; Krebs!

V. crenulata Ch. (V. crenata Gray, V. subrostrata Lmk?
V. eximia Ph., Omphaloclathyrum) station: — ? — ;
habitat: Antillae; Mörch pg. 24! Guadeloupe; Beau

---
*) List of Marine-Shells of the Virgin-Islands. March 63.

pg. 24! Jamaica; Ad.! Virgin-Islands; Swift! St. Thomas; Krebs!

V. cubaniana d'Orb. station: — ? — ; habitat: Cuba; Florida; Martinique; d'Orb.! St. Thomas? Swift! remark: Moll. de Cuba 2—278 pl. 26, fig. 44—46.

V. Dione L. (Dione Gray) station: — ? —; habitat: Antillae; Mörch pg. 27! Trinidad but not at any of the Antilles; d'Orb.! Guadeloupe; Beau pg. 24! Carthagena & Puertorico; Krebs! Carthagena (from Redfield!); Jamaica; Navy-Bay; Ad.!

V. dysera — ? station: — ? — ; habitat: Carthagena (from Redfield!); Ad.! remark: see V. ziczac.

V. flexuosa Linné. station: in sandy mud in creeks with smooth water; habitat: until 39 $\frac{0}{0}$ south; Martinique; Rio Janeiro; La Plata; d'Orb.! Guadeloupe; Beau pag. 24! Carthagena; Jamaica; St. Thomas; Krebs! Jamaica; Ad.! Virgin-Islands; R. Swift! remark: R. Swift in his cat. of Marine shells of the Virgin Isl. places a sign of interogation after „flexuosa", in which he may be correct as the West-Indian shell does not answer in every respect to the description and drawings; he further gives a note of Woodward, according to which the W.-I. shell should be V. punctifera Gray of which Mr. S. has however not been able to find any account.

V. granulata Gm. (V. marica Ch., Cy. lavacrum Bolt.) station: in gravely sand, in creeks with smooth water, close to the surface of the sea and to the shore; habitat: Antillae; Mörch pg. 23! Virgin-Isl.; Swift! Cuba; de la Sagra! Auber! Martinique; Guadeloupe; Candé! Guadeloupe; Beau pg. 24! St. Thomas (Th. Bland); St. Johns (E. Hartwig); Jamaica; Ad.! St. Thomas; St. Johns; Tortola; St. Croix; Carthagena; Krebs!

V. hebraca Lmk. (C. rubiginosa Phil. , C. varians Hanl. by Swift, C. varians Ph. by Beau) station: 7 life specimens from bluish sandy mud in 10 to 12 fathoms water; habitat: Brasils; Mörch pg. 27! Rio-Janeiro; d'Orb.! Martinique; Guadeloupe; Candé! Beau pg. 24! St. Thomas; Krebs! Virgin-Isl.; Swift!

V. inaequivalvis d'Orb. station: — ? —; habitat: Cuba; Auber! Martinique; Florida; d'Orb.! Virgin-Isl.; Swift!

V. Listeri Gray. (Hanley by Swift; Dosina; V. cancellata Ch., Chama persica Meusch., V. puerpera var. 2 Lam. Desh.) station: — ? — ; habitat: Antillae; Mörch pg. 24! Virgin-Island ; Swift!

V. lucinalis Lmk. station: — ? — ; habitat: St. Thomas; Lmk.!

V. mactroides Born. (C. corbicula Gml. Lmk.) station: — ? — ; habitat: Antillae; Mörch pg. 28! Guadeloupe; Cuba; d'Orb.! Guadeloupe; Curaçao; Jamaica; Ad.! St. Juan del Norte de Nicaragua; Chagres; Carthagena; Krebs!

V. maculata L. (Card. tigrinum Mart.) station: — ? — ; habitat: Antillae; Mörch pg. 28! Rio Janeiro; St. Lucia; Martinique; Guadeloupe; Cuba; Jamaica; d'Orb.! Guadeloupe; Beau pg. 24! St. Thomas; Krebs! Tortola; Marecaibo; Jamaica; Ad.! Virgin-Isl.; Swift!

V. minuta Koch. station: — ? — ; habitat: Virgin-Island; Swift!

V. paphia L. (Chione) station: in coarse sand in 1 foot water in creeks with smooth water; habitat: Antillae; Mörch pg. 24! Cuba; de la Sagra! St. Lucy; Martinique; Jamaica; Candé! Guadeloupe; Beau pg. 24! St.

Thomas; Tortola; St. Johns; St. Croix; Carthagena;
Krebs! Jamaica; Ad.! Virgin-Island; Swift!

V. pectorina Lmk. (V. elegans Gray; Timoclea; Leach.)
Brasilia; Mörch pg. 23! West-Indies? Krebs!

V. Philippi d'Orb. (Cyther. concentrica Lmk., C. patago-
nica Phil.) station: — ? — ; habitat: Martinique;
Rio-Janeiro; d'Orb.! remark: Moll. 'de Cuba 2—270.

V. pygmæa Lmk. station: — ? — ; habitat: Antil-
lae; Mörch pg. 24! Guadeloupe; Beau pg. 24! Jamaica;
Ad.! Virgin-Isl.; Swift! St. Johns; St. Thomas; Tortola;
St. Croix; St. Barth; Krebs!

V. rugosa Ch. Gm. (non L., V. rugosa ind. orien. Ch., V.
rigida Sol.; Dillw.) station: — ? — ; habitat: An-
tillae; Mörch pg. 25! Rio Janeiro; d'Orb.! Martinique;
Candé! Guadeloupe; Beau pg. 24! St. Thomas; Tortola;
Jamaica; Ad.! St. Croix; Tortola; St. Johns; Krebs!
Virgin-Islands; Swift!

V. subrostrata Lmk. (V. Bouii Recluz; see V. crenul.)
station: — ? —; habitat: Isl. of St. Johns; Lmk.!

V. trigonella Lmk. station: — ? — ; habitat: Virgin-Isl.; Swift!

V. tripla Linne. station: — ? — ; habitat: Antillae;
Mörch pg. 28! Carthagena; New-Gr.; Krebs!

V. ziczac L. (V. cancellata L., V. cingenda Dw., V. dysera
d'Orb.; V. Lamarckii Gray (Beau) —) station: in lo-
calities like those of V. paphia; habitat: Antillae;
Mörch pg. 24! Brasils; d'Orb.! Martinique & Guadeloupe;
Candé! Beau pg. 24! Jamaica; Ad.! Cuba; de la Sagra!
St. Thomas; Jamaica; Ad.! Virgin-Isl.; Swift! St. Croix;
St. Thomas; St. Johns; Tortola; Puertorico; Carthagena;
Krebs!

Artemis Poli.

A. concentrica Born. (Dosina; Cy. concentrica Link.)
station: — ? — ; habitat: Brasils; Mörch pg. 2≈!
South-Caroline; Virginia; d'Orb.! Guadeloupe; Beau pg.
24! Virgin-Islands; Swift! St. Croix; St. Thomas; Krebs!

A. elegans Con. station: — ? —; habitat: St. Thomas (from Krebs!); Jamaica; South-Caroline; Ad.!

A. tenuis Recluz. (Dosina & Cyclina Recluz, Lycinopsis
Petit) station: in sand, white and fine; about 12 feet
water in the harbour of St. Thomas; habitat: Virgin-
Islands; Swift! St. Thomas; Krebs! Guadeloupe; Beau!
remark: see Journ. de Conch. 185⅜ pg. 250, 1856
pg. 155.

Donax Linné.

D. cayennensis Lmk. station: — ? — ; habitat:
Bahia; St. Lucy; d'Orb.! Guayana; Lmk.!

D. denticulata L. station: in white, fine sand in 2—3
feet water; habitat: Antillae; Mörch pg. 17! Guadeloupe; Beau pg. 25! Virgin-Isl.; Swift! St. Thomas; St.
Croix; Crabisland; St. Johns; Tortola; St. Barth; Trinidad; St. Martha; Carthagena; St. Juan del Norte; Chagres; Krebs!

D. martinicensis Lmk. see Tell. punicea Born.

D. rugosa d'Orb. station: — ? —; habitat: Martinique; Cuba; d'Orb.! Jamaica; Ad.!

D — ? station: — ? —; habitat: Cumana by E. Hartwig; Ad.! Chagres; St. Juan del Norte; Krebs!

Tellina Linné.

T. antillarum d'Orb. station: — ? --; habitat:

Cuba; Auber! Guadeloupe; Beau pg. 25! remark: Moll. de Cuba 2—250 pl. 30 fig. 45—46.

T. Antoni Ph. (Tellinella Gray) station: — ? — ; habitat: Guadeloupe; Beau pg. 25! Antillae; Mörch pg. 13! Virgin-Islands; Swift! remark: a doubtful species.

T. bimaculata L. (T. sexradiata Lmk.; Heterodonax Mörch; Arcopagia d'Orb.) station: in sand close to the shore; habitat: Antillae; Mörch pg. 17! Virgin-Islands; Swift! Cuba; Florida; d'Orb.! Bermuda from Redfield; Jamaica; Ad.! Tortola; St. Croix; St. Thomas; Trinidad; Curaçao; St. Martha; Krebs!

T. brevifrons Say? station: — ? — ; habitat: Jamaica; Ad.!

T. Candeana d'Orb. station: — ? —; habitat: Guadeloupe; Beau pg. 25! Martinique; Candé! Rumkey, Turks-Island (Mrs. A. Holland); Ad.! remark: Moll. de Cuba 2—251 pl. 25 fig. 50—52.

T. caribæa d'Orb. station: — ? — ; habitat: Guadeloupe; Beau pg. 25! Petit! Guadeloupe; Cuba; d'Orb.! remark: Moll. de Cuba 2—250 pl. 30 fig. 47—49.

T. carnaria L. (Strigilla Turton; Lucina carnaria Lmk.) station: in sand close to the shore; habitat: Antillae; Mörch pg. 15! Guadeloupe; Beau pg. 25! Virgin-Isl.; Swift! Brasils; Martinique; Guadeloupe; Cuba; d'Orb.! Jamaica; Ad.! St. Thomas; St. Johns; Tortola; St. Barth; St. Croix; Trinidad; Carthagena; Chagres; Krebs!

T. cayennensis Lmk. (Phammobia) see T. constricta Ph.

T. cerena Ad. station: — ? — ; habitat: St. Johns by E. Hartwig; Jamaica; Ad.!

T. consobrina d'Orb. station: — ? —; habitat: Martinique; d'Orb.! remark: Moll. de Cuba 2—254 pl.

26 fig. 12—14; see Swifts remark to T. subradiata Sch.

T. constricta Phil. (Solen Brug; Phammobia Lmk.) station: — ? — ; habitat: Rio Janeiro; Cuba; d'Orb.! Carthagena by Redfield; Jamaica; Ad.! Nicaragua; Kr.!

T. crystallina Chem. (T. Schrammii Recluz) station: in fine white sand in bays with a strong surf; habitat: Carthagena; Krebs! Redfield! St. Thomas; R. Swift! H. Haagensen!

T. cuneata d'Orb. station: — ? — ; habitat: Guadeloupe; Beau pg. 25! d'Orb.! Cuba; Florida; d'Orb.! remark: Moll. de Cuba 2—256 p. 26 fg. 21—23.

T. decussata Ad. station: — ? — ; habitat: Carthagena (from Krebs!); Jamaica; Ad.!

T. digitalina Lmk. station: supposed to be in rather deep water; habitat: Guadeloupe; Beau pg. 25! Virgin-Islands; R. Swift!

T. exilis Lmk. station: — ? — ; habitat: Guadeloupe; Beau pg. 25! d'Orb.! Petit! Jamaica; Ad.!

T. fausta Soldr. (Arcopagia Leach; T. remies Born non L.; T. laevis Wood); station: in clayish sand close to the shore; habitat: Antillae; Mörch pg. 13! Guadeloupe; Beau! Martinique; St. Lucy; Candé! Cuba; Auber! New-Orleans; Alphen! Virgin-Isl.; Swift! Carthagena (by Redfield); Jamaica; Ad.! St. Thomas; Tortola; Carthagena; Krebs!

T. flexuosa Say (et Sow., T. mirabilis Ph.) station: — ? — ; habitat: Guadeloupe; Beau pg. 25! Guadeloupe; Jamaica; Florida; d'Orb.

T. Gruneri Ph. (T. interstriata Say; T. inornata Ad. acc. to C. B. Ad.) station: in sand in rather deep water in the harbour of St. Thomas; habitat: Virgin-Islands;

Swift! St. Thomas; St. Johns; St. Croix; Krebs! Guadeloupe; Beau pg. 25! remark: Swift says in his „list of marine-shells from the Virgin-Islands": „Mr. Dietz suggests that T. int. Say may be the same; see description in Binneys reprint of Say pg. 125". After the List has been printed, we find a note to the same effect by C. B. Adams, who gives the above synonymes.

T. Guadeloupensis d'Orb. station: — ? — ; habitat: Guadeloupe; Beau pg. 25! d'Orb.! St. Thomas; Swift! remark: Moll. de Cuba 2—252 pag. 26 fig. 1—3.

T. interrupta Solander (T. Listeri Bolt., T. maculosa Lmk.) station: — ? —; habitat: Guadeloupe; Beau pg. 25! Martinique; Candé! Cuba; de la Sagra! Virgin-Isl.; Swift! Bermuda (by Redfield); Tortola; Jamaica; Ad.! St. Thomas; St. Johns; Tortola; Carthagena; Kr.!

T. laevis Ch. (T. laevigata L.) station: — ? — ; habitat: Antillae; Mörch pg. 15! Virgin-Isl.; Swift! Bermuda (by Redfield); Tortola; Ad.!

T. lineata Hanl. (T. lineata Turt., T. brasiliana Lmk.) station: — ? — ; habitat: Rio Janeiro; d'Orbigny! Cuba; Martinique; Candé!

T. magna Spgl. (T. acuta Wood; T. elliptica Lmk.) station: — ? —; habitat: Antillae; Mörch pg. 15! Bermuda; Ad.! Virgin-Islands; Krebs!

T. Martinicensis d'Orb. station: — ? —; habitat: Guadeloupe; Beau pg. 25! d'Orb.! remark: Moll. de Cuba 2—255 p. 26 fig. 15—17.

T. nitens Ad. station: — ? — ; habitat: Jamaica; Adams!

T. pfauperata d'Orb. station: — ? — ; habitat: Guadeloupe; Martinique; d'Orb.! Beau pg. 25! remark: Moll. de Cuba 2—255 p. 26 fig. 18—20.

T. pellucida Ph. station: — ? — ; habitat: Guadeloupe; Beau pg. 25!

T. pisiformis L. (d'Orb.) station: — ? —; habitat: Puertorico; d'Orb.! Guadeloupe; Beau pg. 25! Jamaica; Chagres (by Krebs); Ad.!

T. pudica Hanl. station: — ? — ; habitat: Guadeloupe; Beau pg. 25!

T. punicea Born. (Peronaeoderma Mörch pg. 12, T. angulosa Gm. accord. to Swift, Donax martinisensis Lmk., T. alternata Say & Sowb. acc. to d'Orb., T. striata Ch. acc. to C. B. Ad.) station: in sand outside the surf.; habitat: North-America; Rio-Janeiro; Martinique; Guadeloupe; d'Orb.! Virgin-Isl.; Swift! Surinam; Jamaica; Ad.! Carthagena; Redfield! Krebs! remark: see T. striata Hanl.

T. radiata L. (Musculus; Mörch pg. 13! T. unimaculata Lmk.'; T. nivea Wood) station: in sand on 4 to 6 feet water; habitat: Guadeloupe; Beau pg. 25! Cuba; Martinique; Jamaica; New - Orleans; d'Orb.! Bermuda (by Redfield); Jamaica; Ad.! St. Thomas; St. Croix; St. Johns; Tortola; Trinidad; Carthagena; Krebs!

T. sincera Hanl. station: — ? — ; habitat: Guadeloupe; Beau pg. 25!

T. similis Sow. station: — ? — ; habitat: Antillae; Mörch pg. 14! Martinique; Candé! Virgin-Isl.; Swift!

T. striata Hanl. (non Chem. nec Philippi; Don. martinicensis Lmk. acc. to Swift!) station: — ? —; habitat: Virgin-Islands; Swift! remark: Hanleys R. S. pl. 13 fig. 10 suppl.; Swift says: Hanley in his ill. & desc. cat. of recent shells plate 13 fig. 10 app. page 347 refers Don. mart. to Tellina as T. striata Ch. but the figure vol. x. tab. 170 fig. 1654—55 represents a variety of

T. punicea Born. T. striata H. stands in Beau's Cat. of Guadeloupe shells, but specimens of T. subradiata Schum. have been sent from Guadeloupe (by Beau) as T. striata. See T. punicea Born.

T. Sauleyetiana Recluz. station: — ? —; habitat: Guadeloupe; Beau pg. 25! Virgin-Isl.; St. Thomas in Longbay; Krebs!

T. subradiata Schm. station: — ? —; habitat: St. Thomas (by Krebs); St. Johns (by Hartwig); Ad.! Virgin-Isl.; Swift! remark: Philippi makes T. subradiata Schum. synonyme with T. alternata Say, but Swift thinks them destinct according to the specimens of his collection; we do not see any difference though we have procured authentic north-american specimens of T. alt. Say to compare with West-Indian specimens.

T. vespuciana d'Orb. station: — ? —; Martinique; Jamaica; d'Orb.! remark: Moll. de Cuba 2—254 pl. 26 fig. 12—14.

T. vitrea d'Orb. station: — ? —; habitat: Guadeloupe; Beau pg. 25! d'Orb.! remark: Moll. de Cuba 2—253 pl. 26 fig. 4—5.

Psammobia Lmk.

P. sqvamosa Lmk. station: — ? —; habitat: Virgin-Islands; Swift! remark: very rare.

P. spec. ind. Virgin-Islands; Swift!

Sanguinolaria Lmk.

S. nivea (Solen) Chem. (S. rosea Lmk., Tell. rosea Gm., Sol. sanguinolentus Gm., Sol. fucatus Spgl., Tell. rubicunda Bol., Lobaria rosacea Sch.) station: in sand outside the surf or in the surf; habitat: Cuba; Martini-

que; Guadeloupe; d'Orb.! Marie Galante; Beau pg. 24!
Virgin-Islands; Swift! Jamaica; Ad.! St. Thomas; St.
Croix; Tortola; Carthagena; Trinidad; Krebs!

Capsa Bruguiére.

C. coccinea (Cardium) Martyn. (C. eflorata in d'Orb., Tell.
anomale Ch. Bolt., Corbula radiata Bolt., Caps. rugosa
var. Lmk., Sang. rugosa Blv., S. rug. v. 2 Anton., Asa-
phis) station: in coarse sand in creeks where the water
is smooth; habitat: Florida; Cuba; Martinique; Guadeloupe; St. Lucy; d'Orb.! Carthagena & Bermuda (by
Redfield); Jamaica; Ad.! Virgin-Islands; Swift! St. Thomas; St. Johns; St. Croix; Tortola; Carthagena; Krebs!
remark: Mörch pg. 9!; Beau pg. 24 says: it is not
eatable. But this is a mistake; it is often in the market
of St. Thomas.

Mactra L.

M. alata Wood. (M. carinata Lmk., M. striatula „L." Hanley) station: in sand outside a strong surf at Carthagena; habitat: Brasils; Mörch pg. 4! Virgin-Islands;
Puertorico; Venezuela; Swift! Jamaica; Ad.! Carthagena; Krebs!

M. donacaeformis Gray. (Mulinia) station: — ? — ;
habitat: Nevis; Gray! remark: we think it synonyme
witk M. guad. Recl.

M. guadeloupensis Recl. station: — ? — ; habitat:
Guadeloupe; Beau pg. 26! Guaivia on the coast of Venezuela in Swifts collection; Blume!

Donacilla Lmk. (Mesodesma Desh.)

D. rosea d'Orb. station: — ? — ; habitat: Martinique; Candé! remark: described in Moll. de Cuba 2—238 pl. 25 fig. 39—41.

Semele Sch. (Amphidesma Lmk.)

S. cancellata d'Orb. (A. canc. Sow.) station: — ? —; habitat: Guadeloupe; Martinique; d'Orb.! Guadeloupe; Marie Galante; Beau! Virgin-Islands; Swift! St. Thomas; Krebs! remark: Beau pg. 25; Moll. de Cuba 2—241 pl. 25 fig. 42—44.

S. decussata Wood. (Tellina Wood, A. Jayanum Ad.) station: — ? —; habitat: Virgin-Isl.; Swift! Guadeloupe; Beau! St. Johns (by E. Hartwig); St. Thomas (by Bland) & Jamaica; Ad.! remark: Wood in G. C. 160 pl. 43 fig. 2—3 and Ind. test. p. 28 pl. 4 fig. 81; Ad. in proc. Bost. Soc. N. H. 2 pg. 10.

S. formosum Sowb. station: — ? —; habitat: St. Johns (by E. Hartwig); Jamaica; Ad.!

S. purpurascens Gm. (Venus Gm.; A. variegata Lmk.; Tellina obliqua Wood.) station: — ? —; habitat: Antillae; Mörch! Virgin-Isl.; Swift! Rio-Janeiro; Cuba; Martinique; Guadeloupe; d'Orb.! Guadeloupe; Beau! St. Thomas; Krebs! remark: Wood in Ind. test. pg. 22 Hanley's ed.; Mörch pg. 16; Beau pg. 25.

S. reticulata Lmk. (Tellina Lmk.; Lucina reticulata Lmk.) station: — ? —; habitat: Antillae; Mörch! Guadeloupe; Beau! Virgin-Islands; Swift! Rio Janeiro; Cuba; Martinique; d'Orb.! St. Thomas; Portoplata; Krebs! remark: Chem. vol. 6 fig. 118; Mörch pg. 15; Beau pag. 25.

S. subtruncata Sow. station: — ? —; habitat: Guadeloupe; Beau! Virgin-Isl.; Swift!

Cumingia Sowb.

C. Antillarum d'Orb. station: in crevices on the lower part of madrepores in 8 to 10 feet water; habitat: Virgin-Islands; Swift! Jamaica; Ad.! St. Thomas; Swift! Bland! J. Knox! Krebs! Guadeloupe; Beau! St. Domingo; d'Orb.! remark: Moll. de Cuba Lavignon 2—236 pl. fig. 36—38.

C. lineata d'Orb. station — ? — ; habitat: North-America until Brasils; d'Orb.!

C. sinuata A. Adams. station: — ? — ; habitat: St. Thomas; A. H. Riise! remark: is this not synome with C. Ant. d'Orb.?

C. Petitiana d'Orb. station: — ? —; habitat: Guadeloupe; d'Orb.! Beau pg. 251 remark: see Scrobicularia; Moll. de Cuba 2—236 pl. 25 fig. 33—35.

Scrobicularia Schumacher. (Lavignon; d'Orbigny! Cumingia; Sowb.)

Cyclas Bruguiére.

C. maritima d'Orb. station: in mudy lagoons; habitat: Cuba; Auber! St. Thomas; Swift! remark: Moll. de Cuba 2—280 pl. 26 fig. 47—60.

Glauconome Gray.

G. sp. ind. station & habitat: in the creeks and lagoons by Carthagena, N. Gr.; Krebs!

Saxicava Fleurian de Bellevue.

S. minuta Guild. station: in a crevice of a dead madrepore; habitat: St. Croix; A. H. Riise! St. Thomas; Krebs!

Petricula Lmk.

P. divaricata Ch. station: in crevices on madrepores; St. Thomas; Virgin-Isl.; Swift! remark: Swift says it distinguishes itself by purple syphons from P. lapicida Ch., which has yellow syphons; see P. lapicida Ch. vol. 10 tab. 172 fig. 1666 — 67, Woods Ind. test. pl. 8 fig. 73, Sowb. Tes. pl. 146 fig. 24—25.

P. lapicida Chem. (Venus Chem., P. costata Gray & Lmk., P. divaricata Chem., Ven. divergens Gm., Pr. lucinalis Lmk.) station: in crevices on dead madrepores; habitat: Australia; Sowb.! St. Thomas; Swift! Krebs! St. Domingo; Cuba; Martinique; d'Orb.! Antillae; Mörch! remark: we have a large number of specimens, but are not able to distinguish the shells of P. div. & lap.; Swifts remark about the syphons (see P. div.) are very interesting, but perhaps the colour of the syphons varies by the same species.

P. pholadiformis Lmk. station: — ? — ; habitat: United States; Cuba; d'Orb.!

P. roccellaria Lmk. station: — ? — ; habitat: St. Thomas (by J. H. Newton); Jamaica; Ad.!

P. typica (Chloristodon) Jonas. station: in crevices and holes in Madrepores on 2 to 10 feet water; habitat: Antillae; Mörch pg. 20! Virgin-Islands; Swift!

Anatinacea.

Periploma Schum.

P. inæqvivalvis Schum. station: — ? — ; habitat: Marie Galante; Beau pg. 25!

Thracia Leach. (Blainv. 1824).

T. rugosa Conrad. station: — ? — ; habitat: Rio Janeiro; d'Orb.!

T. plicata? Desch. (T. undata or undulata in Cumings Collection) station: in sand on about 8 to 20 feet water; habitat: Virgin-Islands; Swift! St. Thomas; Tortola; Krebs! remark: Encycl. meth. vol. 3, pg. 1039.

T. sp. ind. station: — ? —; habitat: Virgin-Islands; Swift! remark: like Phaseolina.

Magdala Leach. (Lyonsia Turton; Osteodesma Desh.)

M. Beauiania d'Orb. station: — ? —; habitat: Antillae; d'Orb.! Guadeloupe; Beau! remark: Moll. de Cuba 2—225 pl. 25 lig. 26—28; Beau pg. 26! Deshayes 1827.

M. sp. ind. station: — ? —; habitat: Virgin-Islands; Swift!

Corbulacea.
Corbula Bruguiére.

C. Barrattiana Ad. station: — ? —; habitat: Jamaica; Ad.! remark: desc. in Contr.

C. Blandiana Ad. station: — ? —; habitat: Jamaica; Ad.! remark: desc. in Contr.

C. caribæa d'Orb. station: numerous in mud on 6 fathoms water together with a few specimens of C. Kjæriana; habitat: Cuba; Auber! St. Domingo; Candé! St. Thomas; Krebs! remark: Moll. de Cuba 2—284 pl. 27 lig. 5—8; Encycl. meth. pl. 230, 1792.

C. cubaniana d'Orb. station: — ? —; habitat: Cuba; Auber! Guadeloupe; Beau! remark: moll. de Cuba 2—283 pl. 26 fig. 51—54.

C. Chyttiana Ad. station: — ? —; habitat: Jamaica; Ad.! remark: Described in Contr.

C. Dietziana Ad. station: — ? — ; habitat: Jamaica; Ad.! remark: Descr. in Contr.

C. disparalis d'Orb. station: — ? — ; habitat: Jamaica; Martinique; Guadeloupe; Cuba; d'Orb.! remark: Moll. de Cuba 2—283 pl. 27 fig. 1—4.

C. duplex Ad. station: — ? — ; habitat: Jamaica; Ad.! remark: desc. in Contr.

C. elliptica Recl. station: — ? — ; habitat: Guadeloupe; Beau pg. 26!

C. Kjæriana Ad. station: — ? — ; habitat: Jamaica; St. Juan de Nicaragua (by Krebs); Ad.! St. Thomas; Krebs! remark: desc. in contr.

C. Knoxiana Ad. station: — ? — ; habitat: Jamaica; Ad.! remark: descr. in contr.

C. Krebsiana Ad. station: numerous on 10 to 12 fathoms water together with a few C. caribæa d'Orb.; habitat: Jamaica; Ad.! St. Thomas; Krebs! remark: descr. in contr.

C. Lavelleana d'Orb. station: in mud on 12 feet water; habitat: Jamaica; Martinique; Guadeloupe; Cuba; d'Orb.! Virgin-Islands; Swift! St. Thomas; Krebs! remark: describsd in moll. de Cuba 2—284 pl. 27 fig. 9—12.

C. nitens Turton. (Ervilia, Mya nitens Laskey, Amphidesma purpurascens Lmk. No. 14) station: — ? — ; habitat: Antillae; Mörch! St. Thomas; Tortola; Krebs! Virgin-Islands; Swift! remark: descr. Turtons B. B. pg. 55 pl. 19 fig. 4.

C. Newtoniana Ad. station: — ? — ; habitat: Jamaica; Ad.! St. Thomas; Th. Bland! remark: descr. in Contr.

C. operculata Phil. station: one specimen dredged in

May 1860 in bluish sandy mud on 10 to 12 fathoms
water; habitat: St. Croix; Mörch pg. 30! Virgin-Isl.;
Swift! St. Thomas; Krebs!

C. qvadrata Hinds (Eucharis Recl.) station: — ? — ;
habitat: Antilles; d'Orb.! Guadeloupe; Beau pag. 26!
St. Thomas; Th. Bland! Krebs! Porto - Plata; Krebs!
Virgin - Islands; Swift! remark: Hinds Z. P. 1843,
Reeve Conch. icon. sp. 40, Jour. de Conch. 1850 pg. 168.

C. Swiftiana Ad. station: — ? — ; habitat: Jamaica; Ad.! St. Thomas; Bland! remark: described in
Cont.; several of the Jamaica species are identic with
d'Orbigny's species.

Neaera Gray. (Sphena Turton acc. to d'Orb.)

N. alternata d'Orb. station: — ? — ; habitat: Martinique; d'Orb.! remark: desc. in Moll. de Cuba 2—286
pl. 27 fig. 17—20.

N. cleryana d'Orb. station: — ? — ; habitat: Jamaica; Cuba; St. Thomas; Guadeloupe; d'Orb.! remark: desc. Moll. de Cuba 2—285.

N. ornatissima d'Orb. station: dredged 4 specimens in
May 1860 in bluish-sandy mud from 10 to 12 fathoms
water; habitat: Guadeloupe; Martinique; Cuba; St.
Thomas; d'Orb.! St. Thomas; Swift! Krebs! remark:
desc. in Moll. de Cuba 2—286 pl. 27 fig. 13—16.

Myacea.
Pholadomya G. B. Sowerby 1823.

P. candida Sowb. station: St. Thomas harbour in sand
on 10 to 20 feet water about 40 to 60 feet from the
shore; habitat: Tortola; Mörch pg. 5! Guadeloupe;
Beau pg. 26! St. Thomas; E. Hartwig! Dr. Ravn! Vir-

gin-Islands; Swift! Tortola; St. Thomas; Krebs! remark: desc. in Gen. of shells No 19 fig. 184.

Solenacea.
Solen Linné 1758.

S. bidentatus Spgl. (Tagelus Gray, Siliqvaria Sch., Macha
Gray, S. bidens Ch., S. divisus Fabr, S. fragilis Sol.,
Pult, S. tenuis Wood Sup.?) station: lives in sand close
to the shore even at places where the sand remained dry when
low-water and in mud on 10 to 12 fathoms water; habitat: Antillae; Mörch pg. 8! Martinique; Candé! Guadeloupe; Beau pg. 26! Jamaica; Ad.! Virgin-Islands;
Swift! St. Thomas; St. Croix; St. Johns; Trinidad; Carthagena; St. Juan de Nicaragua; Krebs!

S. lucidus Spgl. (Siliqua Meg., Machaera Gould, Aulus
Oken, Liguminaria Sch., Solecurtoides Desmoulins) station: — ? — ; habitat: America centralis; Mörch
pag. 7!

S. obliquus Spgl. (S. ambiguus Lmk.; Solena Browne)
station: in sand close to the shore; habitat; Cuba;
Sagra! Puertorico; Mörch! Martinique; Candé! Guadeloupe; Beau! Jamaica; Ad.! Virgin-Isl.; Swift! Porto-
Plata; St. Thomas; Puertorico; Krebs! remark: Lmk.
No 7, Hanleys R. S. pg. 13, Woods Ind. test. sup. pl.
11 fig. 17.

S. gibbus Spgl. (S. caribæus Lmk., Siliqvaria notata Sch.,
Baphia coerulescens Meusch?) station: — ? — ; ha-
bitat: Antillae; Mörch pg. 8! Cuba; d'Orb.! North-
Bedford in Mass.; Florida; Cuba; Ad.! Arecibo; J. H.
Newton! Virgin-Islands; Swift! St. Thomas; Carthagena;
St. Juan de Nicaragua; Krebs! remark: Mollusques de
Cuba 2—231.

Psammosolea Risso. (Solecurtis Desh.)

P. Sanctae Marthae Ch. (Solen Ch.) station: in sand
not very distant from the shore; habitat: Antilles;
d'Orb.! Guadeloupe; Beau pg. 26! Virgin-Islands; Swift!
St. Thomas; Tortola; Krebs! remark: Moll. de Cuba
2—232 pl. 25 fig. 31—32.

Pholadea.

Pholas Linné.

P. campechensis Gml. station: found dead on the
sandy beach; habitat: Carthagena; Krebs!

P. candeana d'Orb. station: — ? —; habitat: Martinique; Candé! Havana; Sagra! Florida; d'Orb.! remark: Moll. de Cuba 2—215 pl. 25 fig. 18—19.

P. caribæa d'Orb. station: — ? — ; habitat: Cuba;
Sagra! Mexico; Pet. de Saussaye! Virgin-Islands; Swift!
St. Thomas; Krebs! remark: Moll. de Cuba 2—216
pl. 25 fig. 20—22.

P. corticaria Sowb. station: — ? — ; habitat: Jamaica; Ad.!

P. costata (L.) Gray. station: — ? —; habitat: Antillae; Mörch pg. 3! Cuba; New-Orleans; d'Orb.! North-
Bedford in Mass; Florida; Ad.! Mayaguez; Swift!

P. Hornbecki d'Orb. (P. Beauiana Recl.) station: — ?
habitat: St. Thomas; Hornbeck! Guadeloupe; Beau
pg. 27! Virgin-Islands; Swift! remark: Moll. de Cuba
2—217 pl. 25 fig. 23—25, Journ. de Conch. 1853 pg.
49 pl. 2 fig. 1—3.

P. Krebsii Ad. station: — ? — ; habitat: St. Thomas (by Krebs); Ad.! remark: by us supposed to be
P. striata L.

P. pusilla L. station: in wood close to the shore; ha-

bitat: Rio-Janeiro; Cuba; d'Orb.! St. Thomas?; Kr.!
remark: see P. striata L.

P. striata L. (Martesia Leach, Ph. pusilla L., Ph. clavata
Lmk.) station: in wood in the surface of the water;
Antillae; Mörch pg. 2! Virgin-Isl.; Swift! Guadeloupe;
Beau pg. 27! St. Thomas; Charthagena; Krebs! re-
mark: Woods Ind. test. tab. 2 fig. 7.

Teredo L.

T. navalis L. station: in wood in the surface of the
sea; habitat: Cuba; Auber! St. Thomas; Krebs!

T. norvegica Spgl. station: in wood; habitat: Guadeloupe; Beau pg. 27!

Gastrochaenacea.

Gastrochaena Spengler 1783.

G. hians (Pholas) Ch. (Rocellaria Fl. de Belly, Trapezium
Blv., G. cuneiformis Phil. non Spgl. fide Mörch, Fistulana
rupestris Bosc., G. truncata? Sowb.) station: in life
madrepores from the surface of the sea until on 20 feet
water; habitat: Antillae; Mörch pg. 1! Guadeloupe;
Beau pg. 27! Virgin-Isl.; Swift! St. Domingo; Cuba;
Martinique; St. Thomas; d'Orb.! St. Thomas; St. Croix;
Krebs! remark: its tubes sometimes 8 to 10 inches
long.; Chem. vol. 10 tab. 172 fig. 1678—79; Wood's
Ind. test. pl. 2 fig. 11, Moll. de Cuba vol. 2 pg. 228,
Hanley's Ed. fig. Woods Ind. test. pl. 2 fig. 114 text.,
Wood's Ind. test. supl. pl. 9 fig. 42.

G. ovata.? Sowb. Z. P. 1834. station: — ? — ; habitat: Virgin-Isl.; Swift! remark: Woods Ind. test.
Suppl. pl. 9 fig. 42.

G. rostrata Spgl. (Ph. hians Ch., G. callosa Phil., G.

Chemniziana d'Orb., Rocellaria rostrata Spgl. fide Mörch)
station: in life madrepores until on 20 feet water;
we have never seen the tubes over one inch long; they
are general in pieces of madrepores in which Gast. hians
and several species of the boring lithophagi are living;
habitat: Antillae; Mörch pg. 1! Guadeloupe; Beau pg.
27! St. Thomas by Dr. Hornbeck acc. to d'Orb.! Virgin-Islands; Swift! St. Thomas; Tortola; St. Croix; Kr.!
remark: Moll. de Cuba 2—229 pl. 25 fig. 29—30,
Chem. vol. 10 tab. 172 fig. 1680—81, Jonas Zeits. für
Mal. 1844 pg. 136.

Cardiacea.
Cardium Linné 1758.

C. antillarum d'Orb. (C. graniferum Brod.) station: in
sand between the roots of sea-weed; habitat: Virgin-
Islands; Swift! Guadeloupe; Beau pg. 23! Cuba; Guadeloupe; Martinique; Jamaica; d'Orb.! remark: Moll.
de Cuba 1846 2—309 pl. 27 fig. 53—55, Sowb. 2 pg.
vol. 4—346, Reeve Conch. icon 1844; Swift says: Bro-
derips name was first published & should have precedence.

C. citrinum Ch. (Liocardium Sws., C. triste L.?, C. ser-
ratum Ch. non L., C. hiatus Meuschen, C. lineatum Gm.,
O. laevigatum Lmk.) station: in sand between see-weed;
habitat: Antillae; Mörch pg. 35! Guadeloupe; Beau
pg. 23! Rio Janeiro; Cuba; Martinique; St. Lucy; Guadeloupe; d'Orb.! Bermuda (by Redfield); Jamaica; Ad.!
Virgin-Islands; Swift! St. Thomas; Tortola; five varieties
from Hamsbluff at St. Croix; Trinidad; Krebs!

C. isocardia L. (Trachycardium Mörch pg. 34, Pectunculus Mart.) station: — ? — ; habitat: Antillae;
Mörch! Guadeloupe; Beau pg. 23! Cuba; Sagra! Mar-

tinique; St. Lucy; d'Orb.! Jamaica; Carthagena (by Redfield); Ad.! Virgin-Islands; Swift! St. Thomas; St. Croix;
Tortola; St. Johns; Trinidad; Krebs!

C. laevigatum L. (Reeve, C. pristis Valenc) station:
— ? — ; habitat: St. Thomas; Mörch pg. 35! Guadeloupe; Beau! Margarita; d'Orb.! St. Thomas; Tortola;
Ad.! Virgin-Islands; Swift! St. Thomas; St. Croix; Tortola; Krebs!

C. leucostomum Born. (C. marmoreum Lmk.) station:
— ? — ; habitat: Antillae; Mörch pg. 34!

C. medium L. (Fragum Bolt., Hemicardium Sws.) station:
— ? — ; habitat: Antillae; Mörch pg. 36! Guadeloupe; Beau pg. 23! Florida; Cuba; Martinique; St.
Lucy; d'Orb.! Jamaica; St. Thomas; Carthagena; Ad.!
Virgin-Isl.; Swift! St. Thomas; Tortola; St. Croix; Crabisland; St. Johns; Krebs!

C. muricatum L. station: in sand between Zostera in
1 to 4 feet water; habitat: Antillae; Mörch pg. 34!
Guadeloupe; Beau pg. 23! Rio Janeiro; Cuba; Martini-
que; Guadeloupe; Jamaica; d'Orb.! Carthagena; Jamaica;
South-Caroline; Ad.! Puertorico; Virgin-Islands; Swift!
Krebs !

C. oviputamen Reeve. station: — ? — ; habitat:
Carthagena (by Krebs); Ad.!

C. Petitianum d'Orb. (C. ringiculum Sowb.) station:
in sand between Zostera; habitat: Guadeloupe; d'Orb.!
Beau pg. 23! St. Vincent; Guilding; Virgin-Isl.; Swift!
St. Thomas; St. Johns; Tortola; Krebs! remark: moll.
de Cuba 2—309 pl. 27 fig. 50—52, Sowb. Z. L. 1840,
Conch. icon. spg. 115; Swift says: Sowerby's name should
be retained as it was published long before d'Orbignys.

C. spinosum Meusch. (Papyridea Sws., Solen bullatus Ch.

non Linné , C. soleniforme Brug. , C. bul. pars Lmk.)
station: in sand on shallow water; habitat: Antillae;
Mörch pg. 33! Guadeloupe; Beau pg. 23! Cuba; Mar-
tinique; St. Lucy; Guadeloupe; d'Orb.! Tortola; Jamaica;
Ad.! Virgin-Islands; Swift! Trinidad; Carthagena; Kr.!
C. subelongatum Sow. station: — ? — ; habitat:
Guadeloupe; Beau pg. 23! St. Thomas; Cuba; Martini-
que; d'Orb.! Virgin-Isl.; Swift! Hamsbluff at St. Croix;
Krebs!

Chamacea.
Chama L.

Ch. arcinella L. (Arcinella spinosa Schm.) station: often
on Strombus pug. between seaweed on 8—10 feet water;
habitat: Antillae; Mörch pg. 37! Guadeloupe; Beau
pg. 23! Guadeloupe; Martinique; Cuba; d'Orb.! Jamaica;
Ad.; Virgin-Islands; Swift! St. Thomas; St. Croix; Tortola; Krebs! remark: when young moving about.
Ch. ferruginea Reeve. station: in mud about 2 feet water in creeks; habitat: Antillae; Mörch pg. 37! Virgin-Islands; Swift! St. Thomas; St. Johns; Tortola; Trinidad; Krebs!
Ch. florida Lmk. station: on rocks; habitat: Guadeloupe; Beau pg. 23! St. Domingo; Lmk! Virgin-Isl.;
Swift! St. Thomas; St. Croix; St. Barth; Crabisland; Kr!
Ch. frondosa Brod. station: — ? — ; habitat: Guadeloupe; Beau pg. 23!
Ch. macrophylla Ch. (Ch. bicornis L., Ch. imbricata Lmk.)
station: in mud close to the shore; habitat: Antillae;
Mörch pg. 36! Cuba; Martinique; Guadeloupe; St. Domingo; St. Lucy; d'Orb.! Jamaica; Puertorico; Bermuda;
Ad.! Virgin-Islands; Swift! Krebs!

Ch. radians Lmk. station: — ? — ; habitat: Guadeloupe; Beau pg. 23!

Ch. sarda Reeve. station: fastened on rocks and accord.
to Beau on Strombus gigas; habitat: Antillae; Mörch
pg. 37! Guadeloupe; Beau pg. 23! Virgin - Isl.; Swift!
St. Thomas; St. Johns; St. Barth; Trinidad; Krebs!

Ch. sordida Reeve? station: — ? — ; habitat: Cen-
tral-America; Mörch pg. 37!

Ch. variegata Reeve. station: — ? —; habitat: Virgin-Islands; Swift!

Ch. venosa Reeve. station: — ? — ; habitat: — ?
— ; Guadeloupe; Beau pg. 23!

Ch. 3 sp. not determ. in the collection of R. Swift Esq.;
they are from the Virgin-Islands.

Lucinacea.

Lucina Bruguiére 1792.

L. americana Ad. station: — ? — ; habitat: St.
Thomas (by J. H. Newton); Jamaica; Ad.! remark:
see contributions. = *Diplodonta*

L. aurantia Desh. (V. pens. var. Ch.) station: in sand
on 4 to 6 feet water, where the wind plays freely with
the waves; habitat: Antillae; Mörch pg. 32! Guadeloupe; Beau pg. 23! Virgin - Islands; Swift! common at
Smithsbay, St. Thomas; St. Croix; Krebs! remark:
Chem. vol. 7 fig. 396.

L. Candeana d'Orb. station: — ? —; habitat: Guadeloupe; Martinique; d'Orb.! Guadeloupe; Beau pg. 23!
Virgin-Isl.; Swift! remark: Moll. de Cuba 2—299 pl.
27 fig. 43—45.

L. caribaea d'Orb. station: — ? —; habitat: Guadeloupe; Beau pg. 23! *sp. indet.?*

C. chrysostoma Meuschen (Loripes Poli, V. edentula Ch., Anodonta alba Link., L. Philippiana Reeve) station: in sand on shallow water in creeks; habitat: Florida; Cuba; Martinique; d'Orb.! Puertorico; Jamaica; Ad.! Carthagena; St. Thomas; St. Croix; Tortola; Puertorico; Krebs! Virgin-Isl.; Swift! remark: Chem. 7—427—29; Phill. Abb. pt. 3 pl. 1 fig. 2; Swift observes: the shell Phill. refers to L. edent. is in Conch. icon. sp. 23 L. Phillipiana Reeve; d'Orbigny draws the attention to the marvelous hurry with which this spec. & they L. jamaicensis breed; it is used as food.

L. costata d'Orb. (L. textilis Ph., L. antillarum Reeve, L. ornata Ad.) station: — ? —; habitat: Rio Janeiro; Havana; St. Thomas; Guadeloupe; Jamaica; d'Orb.! Jamaica; Ad.! St. Thomas; St. Croix; Krebs! Virgin-Isl.; Swift! remark: see pilula Ad.

L. digitalis Lmk. (T. pisiformis L.) station: — ? —; habitat: Virgin-Islands; Swift!

L. flexuosa d'Orb. station: — ? —; habitat: Guadeloupe; Beau pg. 23!

L. granulosa C. B. Ad. (L. semireticulata d'Orb.) station: — ? —; habitat: Jamaica; St. Thomas; Ad.! remark: Moll. de Cuba 2—297; is this not L. antillarum Reeve?

L. janeiroensis? Reeve. station: — ? —; habitat: Jamaica; St. Thomas (by Krebs); Ad.!

L. jamaicensis Spgl. (Codakia Scopoli) station: in sand in smooth water; habitat: Antillae; Mörch pg. 32! Guadeloupe; Beau pg. 23! Rio - Janeiro; Martinique; Cuba; Jamaica; d'Orb.! St. Thomas; St. Croix; St. Johns; Carthagena; St. J. Nicaragua; Tortola; Krebs! Jamaica;

Ad.! Virgin-Isl.; Swift! remark: Chem. 7 pg. 409; used as food; d'Orbigny remarks: it breeds very fast.

L. obliqua Reeve non Phill. (L. pectinata C. B. Ad., L. pecten Reeve, L. occidentalis Reeve) station: — ? —; habitat: Virgin-Islands; Swift! remark: Swift says: Adams name has the precedence if it is synonyme and L. obl. Ph. is quite distinct from L. obl. R.; Contributions pg. 245 Nov. 185], Catalogue of N.|A. shells January 1847, Conch. Icon. June 1850 sp. 42 & Aug. 1850.

L. pecten Lmk. (L. imbricatula C. B. Ad. acc. to Beau pg. 23, L.) station: in coarse sand on one foot water in a creek; habitat: Jamaica; Ad.! Antillae; Mörch pg. 33! Guadeloupe; Beau pg. 23! St. Thomas; Tortola; Krebs! remark: Contributions.

L. pensylvanica (Venus) L. (Codakia Scop.) station: in sand close to the shore in shallow water; May 60 dredged 7 specimens of one line diameter in 6 fattoms water on bluish sandy mud; habitat: Antillae; Mörch pg. 32! Guadeloupe; Beau pg. 23! Virgin-Isl.; Swift! Jamaica; Yucatan; Ad.! New-Orleans; Martinique; Cuba; St. Thomas; d'Orb.! St. Thomas; St. Croix; St. Johns; Tortola; Krebs!

L. pilula Ad. (L. costata d'Orb.?) station: — ? —; habitat: St. Thomas (by Krebs); Ad.!

L. punctata (Venus) L. station: — ? —; habitat: Antillae; Mörch pg. 33!

L. qvadrisulcata d'Orb. (Cyclas Klein, Strigrilla Gray, T. divaricata Ch.) station: — ? —; habitat: Antillae; Mörch pg. 32! Guadeloupe; Beau pg. 32! Virgin-Isl.; Swift! Krebs! remark! Beau gives as synonymes L. div. L. & L. dentata Wood, but L. qvadrisul

d'Orb. as a separate species; Moll. de Cuba 2—292 pl.
27 fig. 34 – 36, Chem. vol. 6—129 fide Mörch.

L. scabra Lmk. (L. scobinata Recl., Tell. muricata Spgl.,
Cyrachæa Leach, Myrtea Turt.?, T. imbricata Chemn.)
station: dredged from 6 to 12 fathoms water in bluish
sandy mud; habitat: Antillae; Mörch pg. 32! Guadeloupe; Beau pg. 23! Martinique; Cuba; Jamaica; St.
Thomas; d'Orb.! Jamaica; Ad.! Virgin-Islands; R. Swift!
St. Thomas; Tortola; St. Croix; Krebs!

L. semireflecta d'Orb. station: — ? — ; habitat:
San Blas in Patagonia; Rio-Janeiro; Cuba; d'Orb.! remark: Moll. de Cuba 2—297.

L. serrata d'Orb. (L. Chemnitzii Ph., L. divaricata Rv.
non L.) station: — ? — ; habitat: St. Thomas (by
J. H. Newton); Ad.! Virgin-Islands; Swift! Cuba; St.
Martin; d'Orb.! Guadeloupe; Beau pg. 23! remark:
Moll. de Cuba 2—295 pl. 27 fig. 37—39, Zeitschrift
1848, Conch. Icon. spec. 47.

L. tigerina L. (Codakia Scop., Chama Mart., Lentilaria
Sch., Cyth. tigerina Lmk) station: in coarse sand between zostera on one foot water in bays and creeks; habitat: Antillae; Mörch pg. 33! Guadeloupe; Beau pag.
23! New-Orleans; Cuba; Martinique; Guadeloupe; St.
Thomas; d'Orb.! Bermuda; Carthagena; Redfield! Virgin-Isl.; Swift! Jamaica; Ad.! Puertorico; St. Thomas;
St. Croix; St. Johns; Carthagena; Trinidad; Krebs! remark: commonly eaten by poor people.

L. trisinuata d'Orb. station: —? — ; habitat: Guadeloupe; Beau pg. 23! Martinique; Guadeloupe; d'Orb.!
remark: Moll. de Cuba 2—300 pl. 27 fig. 46—49.

L. virgo? Reeve. station: — ? — ; habitat: Guade-

loupe; Beau pg. 23! Jamaica; Ad.! Virgin-Islands in the
cabinet of H. Krebs; Swift! ˮ ʄ ˮˑ ˮˑⱯᵌⁱˮ ⁱ Ɐ ᴿ

5 species indetermined from the Virgin-Islands in the cabinet of R. Swift Esq. St. Thomas.

3 species indetermined from the West-Indies in the cabinet
of H. Krebs Esq. St. Thomas.

Fimbria Mergele v. Muchlfeld.

F. magna Meg. (Venus fimbriata L., Gafrarium Bolton,
Corbis Cuv., Idotea perforata Sch.) station: — ? — ;
habitat: Antillae; Mörch pg. 33!

Diplodonto Brown 1831.

D. semiaspera? Ph. station: — ? — ; habitat: Virgin-Islands; Swift!

D. species indetermined. Virgin-Islands; Swift!

Astarteacea.

Crassatella Lmk. 1799 in prodr.

C. antillarum Reeve. (C. rostrata Lmk.?) station: — ?
— ; habitat: Island of Margarita; Mörch pg. 39!

C. martinicensis d'Orb. station: — ? — ; habitat:
Jamaica; Martinique; St. Domingo; d'Orb.! Virgin-Isl.;
Swift! Krebs! remark: Moll. de Cuba 2—288 pl. 27
fig. 21—23.

C. guadaloupensis d'Orb. station: living on madrepores; Beau pg. 22!, under pieces of dead madrepores
in gravely sand on one foot water and dredged in bluish
sandy mud from 10 to 12 fathoms water; habitat:
Cuba; Guadeloupe; St. Domingo; St. Thomas; d'Orb.!
Virgin-Islands; Swift! Krebs!

C. rostrata Lmk. station: — ? — ; habitat: West-
Indies; South America; Lmk.!

Carditacea.

Cardita Bruguiére 1798.

C. domingensis d'Orb. station: — ? — ; habitat: St. Domingo; Cuba; d'Orb.! remark: Moll. de Cuba 2—291 pl. 27 fig. 27—29.

C. gibbosa Rv. station: — ? — ; habitat: Florida; Yucatan; Ad.!

C. ovata Ad. station: — ? — ; habitat: Jamaica; Adams!

C. spec. ind. in the collection of R. Swift Esq. at St. Thomas; he observes in his list of the marine-shells of the Virgin-Islands: „may be C. gracilis Shuttl. who received specimens from Puertorico", but Swift has not the diagnoçis; see Trapezium.

Trapezium Megerle v. Muehlfeld.
(Coralliophaga Blv., Cardita Lmk.)

T. dactylus Brug. (Cardita Brug., Chama coralliophaga Ch., C. carditoidea Blv., Cypricardia Hornbeckiana d'Orb.?) station: on they lower side of madrepores; habitat: Antillae; Mörch pg. 19! St. Thomas; d'Orb.! Guadeloupe; Bean pg. 23! Virgin-Islands; Krebs! St. Thomas; Jamaica; Ad.! remark: Moll. de Cuba 2—266 pl. 26 fig. 33—34.

T. gracilis (Cypricardia) Shuttl. station: — ? — ; habitat: Guadeloupe; Beau pg. 23! remark: we have received specimens from Guadeloupe, which we are not able to distinguish from the former.

Solemyacea.

Solemya Lmk.

S. occidentalis D. station: dredged with bluish sandy

mud on 10 to 12 fathoms water; habitat: Crabisland;
St. Thomas; Krebs! Guadeloupe; Beau! remark: Jcon.
de Conch.

Arcacea.
Arca L. 1758.

A. Adamsi Shuttl. station: in crevices of madrepores;
habitat: Guadeloupe; Beau pg. 22! Virgin-Isl.; Swift!
Tortola; St. Thomas; Porto-Plata; Krebs!

A. americana Gray. (A. pexata Say) station: — ? — ;
habitat: Guadeloupe; Beau pg. 22! Florida; Cuba;
d'Orbigny!

A. antiqvata L. (Anodara Gray, A. Deshaysii Ph., A.
hemidermos Ph.) station: small specimens fastened on
madrepores and old specimens loose in blue sandy mud
on 10 to 12 fathoms water; habitat: Cuba; Martinique; d'Orb.! Jamaica; Cuba; Carthagena; Ad.! Virgin-
Islands; Swift! Krebs!

A. auriculata Lmk. station: — ? — ; habitat: St.
Thomas; Cuba; d'Orb.!

A. barbadensis Petiver station: — ? — ; habitat:
Cuba; St. Lucy; Martinique; St. Thomas; d'Orb.!

A. brasiliana Lmk. (Scapharca Gray) station: — ? —;
habitat: St. Croix; Mörch pg. 41! Guadeloupe; Beau
pg. 22! Rio Janeiro; Martinique; Guadeloupe; Cuba;
d'Orbigny!

A. candida Helbling. (Lithoarca Gray, A. ovata Gmelin.,
A. trapizina Lmk., A. Helbingii Brug.) station: fastened
on the lower side af madrepores; habitat: Antillae;
Mörch pg. 40! Guadeloupe; Beau pg. 22! Florida; Martinique; Cuba; d'Orb.! Jamaica; St. Thomas; Ad.! Virgin-Isl.; Swift! Carthagena; Jamaica; St. Thomas; Tor-

tola; Krebs! remark: Deshayes says in a note in Lmk. an. sans vert. vol. 6 pg. 469: this species should be retained as A. nivea Chem. vol. 7 pg. 538.

A. incongrua Say. station: — ? —; habitat: Navy-Bay; Florida; South Carolina; Carthagena; Ad.! Carthagena?; Krebs!

A. indica Gml. station: — ? — ; habitat: Guadeloupe; Beau pg. 22! Virgin-Isl.; Swift!

A. labiata Sowb. station: — ? —; habitat: Guadeloupe; Beau pg. 22!

A. lactea L. station: — ? — ; habitat: Guadeloupe; Beau pg. 22! Natal Coast; Jamaica; Cicily; St. Thomas; Ad.!

A. Listeri Ph. (Barbatia Gray, A. fusca Brug, A. granulata Meusch.) station: — ? — ; habitat: Antillae; Mörch pg. 40! Cuba; Martinique; Guadeloupe; d'Orb.! St. Thomas; Jamaica; Ad.! Virgin-Islands; Swift! Kr. !

A. noac L. station: in 10 fathoms water in mud, 6—7 attached together and in crevices of large pieces of madrepores; habitat: Guadeloupe; Beau pg. 22! Tortola; St. Thomas; Jamaica; Carthagena; Bermuda; Ad.! Virgin-Islands very common; Krebs! remark: C. B. Ad.s says it is synonyme with A. occidentalis Phil.

A. notabilis Bolt. (Anodara Gray, A. Deshayesii Hanley) station: — ? —; habitat: Antillae; Mörch pg. 41! Guadeloupe; Beau pg. 22! Virgin-Islands; Swift!

A. occidentalis Ph. (Cilota Browne, Daphne Poli, Navicula Blv.) station: as A. noae; habitat: Virgin-Isl.; Swift! Antillae; Mörch pg. 39! remark: see A. noae L.

A. rhombea Born. (A. Chemnitzii Phil., Scapharca) station: in crevices of corals, at the root of gorgoniae and in mud on 10 fathoms water; habitat: Antillae; Mörch

pg. 41! Virgin-Islands; Swift! remark: Chem. vol. 7
fig. 553—56, Zeitsch. 1851 pg. 50.

A. sqvamosa Lmk. (A. gradata Brod., A. donaciformis,
Rv., A. divaricata Sowb., A. domingensis Lmk., Daph-
noderma Mörch, A. angulata Meusch.) station: below
madrepores; habitat: Antillae; Mörch! Guadeloupe;
Beau pg. 22! St. Domingo; Lmk.! St. Thomas; St. Johns;
Ad.! Virgin-Islands; Swift! Krebs!

A. umbonata Lmk. (Cilota Brown, A. ventricosa Lmk.
according to C. B. Ad.! A. imbricata Brug; A. muta-
bilis Reeve, A. americana d'Orb. non Gray) station:
fastened to madrepores and in the roots of gorgoniae;
habitat: Antillae; Mörch pg. 40! Guadeloupe; Beau
pg. 22! Ad.! Virgin-Islands; Swift! Chagres; St. Thomas; Antigua; Jamaica; Carthagena; Ad.! St. Thomas;
St. Croix; Tortola; Krebs! remark: Adams separates
A. umb. from A. imbricata; Moll. de Cuba 2—317 pl.
28 fig. 12 l

Pectunculus Lmk. (Axinaea Poli, Glycimeris da Costa)
station: we are not able to give the station of any of
the Pectunculi.

P. angulatus Lmk. spec. 8 (Arca angulosa Gml.) habitat: Tortola; Swift!

P. castaneus Lmk. non Reeve. (P. variegatus Chem.)
habitat: Guadeloupe; Beau pg. 22! St. Johns; Jamaica; Ad.!

P. castaneus Reeve non Lmk.; habitat: Tortola; Swift!
Krebs! remark: perhaps Adams habitat refers to this
species.

P. decussatus L. (P. pennaceus Lmk. spec. No 6) habitat: Virgin-Islands; Swift! Tortola; Krebs!

P. hirtus Phil. habitat: Cumana; Philippi Zeitsch. 1846 pg. 191! Isl. of Margaritha; Swift! West-Indies; Krebs!

P. minimus Gml. habitat: St. Thomas; Riise! remark: the name derives from Mörch but the specimens are by us considered the young of P. pectinatus Gm.

P. oculatus Reeve. spec. 38 (P. pectiniformis Lmk. acc. to d'Orbigny) habitat: West-Indies; Reeve! Tortola; Swift! Krebs! Martinique; d'Orb.! Guadeloupe; Beau pg. 22! remark: Reeve's description does not satify us.

P. pectenoides Desh. habitat: Tortola Swift!

P. pectinatus Gml. (Arca Gmel., A. costata Mensch., A. pectunculus minor Ch., P. minor d'Orb.) habitat: Isl. la Plata; Reeve! St. Thomas; Riise! Krebs! Tortola; Carthagena (by Krebs); Ad.! Guadeloupe; Beau pg. 22! Tortola; Swift! Krebs! remark: Riise has d'Orb.'s name from Mörch.

P. scriptus Lmk. habitat: St. Domingo; Lmk.

P. sericatus Reeve spec. 49; habitat: Tortola; Reeve! Swift! Krebs! St. Thomas; Krebs! St. Johns; Ad.! Guadeloupe; Beau pg. 22!

P. spadiceus Reeve. habitat: — ? — ; Reeve! St. Juan del Norte de Nicaragua; Krebs!

P. undatus L. (P. undulatus Lmk. spec. 3, P. lineatus Reeve fide Mörch pg. 42) habitat: Virgin-Isl.; Swift! St. Thomas; Tortola; Krebs! Guadeloupe; Beau pg. 22!

P. spec. ind No 4. habitat: Riise has 2 specimens from Crabisland; Krebs has one valve from St. Martin; remark: it is ineqvilatoral and approaching P. spadiceus, but mustly white with a few brown specks; diameter from 4 to 6 lines.

P. spec. ind. No 2. habitat: Porto-Plata; St. Thomes;

Krebs! remark: two perfect specimens and two odd valves; perhaps young undatus or decussatus or hirtus; remark: are P. hirtus Phil. and P. undatus L. and P. decussatus L. & angulatus L. not synonymes?

Heteromyaria.
Mytilacea.
Mytilus L.

M. exustus L. (M. Domingensis Lmk., d'Orb., Hormomya Mörch) station: on rocks which are over low-water mark; habitat: Antillae; Mörch pg. 53! Guadeloupe; Beau pg. 22! Rio Janeiro; Cuba; Martinique; d'Orb.! Jamaica; St. Thomas; Ad.! Virgin-Islands; Swift; Carthagena; St. Thomas; St. Johns; Krebs! remark: it evelopes itself very differently in places where the sea is smooth and in places where the sea is rough.

M. Lavelleanus d'Orb. station: — ? — ; habitat: Guadeloupe? d'Orb.! remark: Moll. de Cuba 2—328 pl. 28 fig. 3—5.

M. viator d'Orb. station: — ? — ; habitat: Patagonia; Cuba; d'Orb.!

Modiolus Lmk.

M. americana Tarvart d'Herbigny (M. amer. Leach?, M. tulipa Lmk., Perna Adans., Volsella Scop., Pholas Kl.) station: between seaweed on gravel in a few feet water in creeks; habitat: Antillae; Mörch pg. 53! Guadeloupe; Beau pg. 22! Cuba; Martinique; Guadeloupe; St. Lucy; d'Orb.! Jamaica; Bermuda; Ad.! Virgin-Isl.; Swift! all the West-Indian islands from Trinidad to St. Domingo; Krebs!

M. b a r b a t a? L. s t a t i o n: — ? — ; h a b i t a t: North-Bedforth; Jamaica; St. Thomas; d'Orb.!

M. c a s t a n e a Say. s t a t i o n: between sea-weed in coarse sand close to the shore; h a b i t a t: South-Carolina; Jamaica; St. Thomas; Ad.! Florida; on a specimen in the Academy of N. Sc. in Philadelphia! Virgin-Isl.; Swift! St. Thomas; St. Croix; Tortola; Krebs!

M. l i t o r a l i s? Say. s t a t i o n: — ? —; h a b i t a t: Virgin-Islands; Swift!

M. m o d i o l u s L. (Arca L., M. citrinus polydentalus Ch., Tamarindiformis striatus Mensch., M. citrinus Bolt., M. sulcatus Lmk., M. exustus Gml., d'Orb. non L., M. Chemnitzii Pot. & Mich., Brachydontes Sws.) s t a t i o n: on rocks above low-water-mark; h a b i t a t: Antillae; Mörch pg. 54! Guadeloupe; Beau pg. 22! Cuba; d'Orb.! Virgin-Islands; Swift! Krebs!

Lithophagus Megerle v. Muehlfeld.

L. b i s u l c a t u s d'Orb. (Mod. appendiculatus Ph.) s t a t i o n: boring in life madrepores; h a b i t a t: Antillae; Mörch pg. 56! Guadeloupe; Beau pg. 22! Cuba; Jamaica; Martinique; Guadeloupe; St. Domingo; d'Orb.! Virgin-Islands; Swift! Krebs! r e m a r k: Moll. de Cuba 2—333 pl. 28 fig. 14—16; we are in possession of several very interesting specimens, where the animal has been obliged 5—6 times to form concave bases to rest on to be able to keep communication with the sea and to prevent to be overgrown by the madrepores; they are conseqvently able to loose the byssus and to refasten it as they are moving upward; it will be understood that thereby is formed a wedgeformed hole from the centre of the madrepore toward the surface as the animal of the Lithophagus increases in size and the hole is intersected at intervals by the above mentioned, on the upper side concave, on the lower side convex, bases.

L. caribæus Ph. station: — ? — ; habitat: Antillae; Mörch pg. 56!

L. dactylus Sow. (Lithodomus Cuv., L. antillarum d'Orb., L. corrugata Phil.) station: in life madrepores; habitat: Antillae; Mörch pg. 55! Virgin-Isl.; Swift! Cuba; Martinique; Guadeloupe; d'Orb.! remark: Moll. de Cuba 2—332 pl. 28 fig. 12—13.

L. fuscus Gml. (Mytilus brunneus Soldr., Mod. cinnamomea var. Lmk., Mod. Favannii Pot. & Mich., Botula Mörch) station: in life madrepores; habitat: Antillae; Mörch pg. 55! Guadeloupe; Beau pg. 22! Virgin-Islands; Swift! Cuba; Martinique; St. Domingo; Jamaica; d'Orb.! St. Thomas; Jamaica; Lmk.! St. Thomas; St. Croix; Tortola; Krebs!

L. niger Lister. (Pholas Lister, L. antillarum Phil.) station: in madrepores; habitat: Antillae; Mörch pg. 56! Guadeloupe; Beau pg. 22! Cuba; Martinique; St. Domingo; St. Lucy; d'Orbig.! Virgin-Islands; Swift! Krebs! remark: Moll. de Cuba 2—332 pl. 28 fig. 10—11; the Lethophagi are only found alife in the madrepores as long as these are alife.

Dreisenia Beneden.

D. Rissei? ; station: in brackish water between the roots of Avicennia; habitat: Crabisland; Riise! Porto-Plata; Krebs!

Pinnacea.

Pinna L.

P. muricata L. (P. nobilis Ch., P. seminuda Lmk., Pen-

naria Browne, P. rigida Sold.) station: in mud and sand
on 1 to 3 feet water in smooth water; habitat: Cuba;
Martinique; Guadeloupe; d'Orb.! Virgin-Islands; Swift!
Jamaica; St. Thomas; Carthageua; Ad.! Krebs!

P. pernula Ch. (P. haud ignobilis Ch., P. degenera Link.,
P. carnea Gm., P. flabellum Lmk., P. varicosa (Lmk.)
d'Orb., Chimaera Poli) station: as the former; habitat: Antillae; Mörch pg. 51! Guadeloupe; Beau pg. 22!
Cuba; Martinique; Guadeloupe; Trinidad; St. Croix;
d'Orb.! Jamaica; Tortola; St. Thomas; Ad.! Krebs! Virgin-Islands; Swift!

Monomyaria.
Maleacea.
Avicula Bruguiére.

A. Candeana d'Orb. (Malleus Lmk.) station: — ? — ;
habitat: Cuba; de Candé! Guadeloupe; Beau pg. 21!
remark: Moll. de Cuba 2—343 pl. 28 fig. 25—27.

A. colymbus Bolton. (A. Pteria Scop., Glaucus Poli,
Anomica Oken, M. Hirundo Ch., A. atlandica Lmk., A.
communis Lmk.) station: at the root of Gorgoniae,
habitat: Antillae; Mörch pg. 51! Jamaica; St. Thomas; Tortola; Ad.! Virgin-Islands; Swift!

A. crocata Swains. station: — ? — ; habitat: Jamaica; St. Johns; St. Thomas; Carthagena; Tortola; Ad.!

A. guadelupensis d'Orb. station: — ? — ; habitat: Guadeloupe; Beau pg. 21! d'Orb.! remark: Moll.
de Cuba 2—343 pl. 28 fig. 23—24.

A. heteroptera Lmk. station: — ? — ; habitat: Antillae; Mörch pg. 51!

A. longisqvamosa Dunk. station: — ? — ; habitat
Guadeloupe; Beau pg. 21!

A. macroptera Lmk. station: — ? — ; habitat: Guadeloupe; Beau pg. 21! Virgin-Islands; Swift!

A. radiata Leach. (Margaritifera Browne; Meleagrina Lmk., A. guadeloupensis d'Orb. according to Beau pg. 21) station: — ? — ; habitat: Antillae; Mörch pg. 50!

Melina Retz. (Isognomum Kl., Isogonum Bolt., Perna Lmk.).

M. alata Gm. (Ostrea Gm., Sutura Meg., Ala corvi pendula Ch., Riparia isogoalata Mensch., Perna obliqua Lmk.) station: in large clusters in creeks with stones and smooth water; habitat: Antillae; Mörch pg. 49! Guadeloupe; Beau pg. 22! Cuba; Martinique; d'Orb.! Jamaica; Ad.! Virgin-Islands; Swift! Krebs! Carthagena; Krebs! remark: is eatable.

M. bicolor Ad. station: — ? — ; habitat: Jamaica St. Johns; St. Thomas; Ad.!

M. perna L. (Concha semiaurita Ch., O. canteriata Mensh., M. perniformis Retz, Perna sulcata Lmk., P. vulcella b Lmk., P. Linnæi Pfr., P. Lamarckiana d'Orb.) station: Antillae; Mörch pg. 49 — 50! Guadeloupe; Beau pg. 22! Martinique; de Candé!

M. vulsella Lmk. P. Lamarckiana d'Orb. accor. to Swift, Concha semiaurita var. Ch., P. Chemnitziana d'Orbigny) station: on rocks at the level of the sea; habitat: Cuba; Martinique; St. Croix; d'Orb.! Virgin-Isl.; Swift! Krebs! Carthagena; Krebs!

Pectinea.
Lima Bruguiére 1792.

L. bullata Born. (Limatula S. Wood) station: — ? — ; habitat: Antillae?; Mörch pg. 57! remark: see L. scabra Born.

L. caribæa d'Orb. (Radula Kl.) station: — ? — ; habitat: Antillae; Mörch pg. 57! Cuba; Auber! remark:
Moll. de Cuba 2—337 pl. 28 fig. 17—19.

L. cubaniana d'Orb. station: — ? — ; habitat: Cuba;
Auber! remark: Moll. de Cuba 2—337 pl. 28 fig.
20—22.

L. inflata Lmk. (L. pellucida Ad.) station: in small caves
in the sand between stones on 1 to 2 feet water; this
species, as well as L. tenera & L. scabra, moves quick
about by opening and shutting the valves; habitat:
Jamaica; St. Thomas; Guadeloupe; Ad.! St. Thomas;
St. Martin; St. Barth; Krebs!

L. multicostata Sowb. station: — ? — ; habitat:
Florida; Jamaica; St. Thomas; St. Johns; Ad.! remark:
Adams says: generally confounded with the mediterranien
species, which is the L. sqvamosa Lmk.

L. scabra Born (Ctenoides Klein, L. aspera Ch., L. glacialis Gm. & Lmk., Limaria asperula Link., Swift gives
as synonymes: O. bullata Born. & L. fragilis Lmk.)
station: see L. inflata; habitat: Antillae; Mörch pg.
57! Guadeloupe; Beau pg. 21! Cuba; Martinique; St.
Lucy; d'Orb.! Jamaica; St. Thomas; Porto-Cabello; St.
Johns; Ad.! Virgin-Islands; Swift! Krebs!

L. squamosa? Lmk. (see L. multicostata Sowb.) station:
— ? — ; habitat: Guadeloupe; Beau pg. 41!

L. tenera Ch. (Ctenoides Klein, Ost. glacialis Solis, Limaria
glacials Lmk.) station: as L. inflata Lmk.; habitat:
Antillae; Mörch pg. 57! Carthagena; Jamaica; Ad.! Virgin-Islands; Krebs!

Pecten O. Fried. Mueller (Rondelet 1606.)

P. antillarum d'Orb. station: — ? —; habitat: Guadeloupe; Beau pg. 21!

P. **exasperatus** Sowb. station: — ? — ; habitat: Antillae; Mörch pg. 59! Virgin-Islands; Swift!

P. **fucatus** Reeve. station: — ? — ; habitat: Virgin-Isl.; Swift!

P. **gibbus** Lmk. station: — ? — ; habitat: Cuba; Martinique; Guadeloupe; d'Orb.!

P. **imbricatus** Gm. (Ostrea Gm., Pera venatoria imbricata Ch.) station: — ? —; habitat: Antillae; Mörch pg. 58! St. Thomas; St. Johns; Ad.! Virgin-Islands; Swift! St. Croix; Trinidad; Tortola; Krebs!

P. **nodosus** L. (C. coralinus Ch. acc. to Bean) station: — ? — ; habitat: Antillae; Mörch pg. 58! Guadeloupe; Bean pg. 21! Cuba; Guadeloupe; Martinique; d'Orb.! St. Thomas; Bermuda; St. Johns; Ad.! Virgin-Islands; Swift! Krebs!

P. **nucleus** Born. (P. turgidus Lmk., Argus Gray) station: — ? — ; habitat: Antillae; Mörch pg. 59! Guadeloupe; Bean pg. 21! Virgin-Islands; Swift!

P. **ornatus** Lmk (Pectinium Link., Chlamys Bolton) station: — ? — ; habitat: Antillae; Mörch pg. 57! Guadeloupe; Bean pg. 21! Florida; Cuba; St. Lucy; d'Orb.! Jamaica; St. Johns; Ad.! St. Thomas; Carupana; Tortola; Krebs! Virgin-Islands; Swift!

P. **Sowerbii** Guild. station: — ? — ; habitat: Florida; Jamaica; St. Thomas; Carthagena; Ad.!

P. **sulcatus** Lmk. No 21 (P. antillarum Recluz) station: — ? — ; habitat: Virgin-Islands; Swift!

P. **ziczac** L. (Vola Klein, Pandora Meg., Janeira Sch.) station: — ? —; habitat: Antillae; Mörch pg. 59! Guadeloupe; Bean pg. 21! Cuba; Martinique; Guadeloupe; St. Lucy; St. Domingo; St. Thomas; Jamaica;

d'Orb.! Tortola; Jamaica; Carthagena; Ad.! Virgin-Isl.; Swift! Krebs!

Spondylus L. (Lister 1686.)

S. americanus Lmk. No 2 (S. folia brassicae Ch., S. gacdcropus Ch. acc. to d'Orb.) station: — ? —; habitat: St. Domingo; Lmk.! Guadeloupe; Beau pg. 21! St. Domingo; Cuba; Martinique; d'Orb.! Virgin-Islands; Swift!

S. coccinus Lmk. station: — ? —; habitat: Guadeloupe; Beau pg. 21! remark: perhaps synonyme with S. fimbr. M.

S. echinatus d'Orb. station: — ? —; habitat: Cuba; Martinique; Guadeloupe; d'Orb.! Virgin-Islands; Swift!

S. fimbriatus Mcusch. (Ostrea spondyloides Gm., S. spatuliferus Lmk. No 13, S. divaricatus Schrit.) station: on rocks in 7 to 10 feet water where the surf is strong; habitat: Bermuda; St. Thomas; Carupano; Ad.! Virgin-Islands; Swift! Krebs!

S. radians Lmk. No 19 station: — ? —; habitat: Virgin-Isl.; Swift!

S. striato-spinosus Ch. station: — ? —; habitat: Jamaica; St. Thomas; Ad.! remark: is this not our S. fimb. M.?

Plicatula Lmk.

P. depressa? Lmk. station: — ? —; habitat: Virgin-Islands; Swift!

P. ramosa Lmk. station: — ? —; habitat: Guadeloupe; Beau pg. 21!

P. spondyloidea Mcusch. (Ostrea Mcusch., Sp. plicatus Ch., P. cristata Lmk., P. reniformis Lmkn-., P. barbades sis (Petiver) d'Orb.) station: on rocks in 7—10 feet water; habitat: Guadeloupe; Beau pg. 21! Antilles Rio - Janeiro; Patagonia d'Orb.! Jamaica: Florida; St. Thomas; Ad.! Virgin-Islands; Swift! Krebs!

Ostreacea.

Ostrea L. 1768.

O. arborea Ch. (Mulleria Fer., O. radicum Ch., O. rhizophorae Ch., O. parasitica Gm.) station: in lagoons and creeks on the root of Avicennia and Rhizophora; habitat: Antillae; Mörch pg. 62! Cuba; Jamaica; Ad.! Guadeloupe; Beau pg. 21! Virgin-Islands; Swift!

O. cristata Born. station: — ? —; habitat: Guadeloupe; Beau pg. 21!

O. frons L. Ch. (O. transtra Mensch., rubella Lmk., limacella Lmk., crucella Lmk., folium (L.) d'Orb.) station: on the roots of trees in lagoons and creeks; habitat: Cuba; Martinique; Guadeloupe; St. Lucy; St. Domingo; New - Orleans; d'Orb.! Guadeloupe; Beau pg. 21! Jamaica; Tortola; Ad.! Virgin-Islands; Swift! Krebs!

O. rostralis Lmk. station: — ? — : habitat: Guadeloupe; Beau pg. 21!

O. spreta d'Orb. station: — ? —; habitat: Rio-Janeiro; Cuba; d'Orb.! remark: moll. de Cuba 2—365 pl. 28 fig. 30.

O. spec. ind. No 1 from St. Croix and Guadeloupe, in the cabinets of R. Swift & H. Krebs; Swift says: it approaches O. cucullata Born in Lmk. an. sans vert. No 34.

Placunanomia Broderip 1832.

P. echinata? Brod. (P. abdominalis Gray) station: between the branches of corals; habitat: Guadeloupe; Beau pg. 21! Virgin-Islands; Swift!

P. rudis Brod. station: nests especially in the dead shells
of Pinna muricata; habitat: Virgin - Islands; Swift!
Krebs!

Anomia L. 1767.

A. simplex d'Orb. station: — ? — ; habitat: Guadeloupe; Beau pg. 211 Martinique; Cuba; d'Orb.! Virgin-Islands; Swift: remark: Moll. de Cuba 2—367 pl.
28 pg. 31—33.

Copy of a letter from the Author.

Copenhagen.
Ole Suhr's Gade 24.
1st December, 1884.

Messrs. R. Friedländer & Sohn,
Berlin.

Dear Sirs,

In reply of your favor dated 29th last month I beg to inform you, that "the West-Indian Marine Shells, with some remarks", 1864, was only printed in 20 copies, of which 3 were - according to the law - delivered to the public Libraries, 7 were lost in transmitting them to St. Thomas, 3 went to the Universities of Sweden and Norway, and a few given to friends.

The work is of very little value, and it was only printed with the view to get it supplied with notes from those friends to whom it was circulated.

I have a copy, with many notes in, and a copy, which consists of the proof-sheets from the printer. These last are very little maculated and as good as a clean copy.

Consequently there are none for sale (my friends tease me that the book is the costliest they know, on account of a copy has been sold in Altona at auction for 10 Rx, it is only 137 pages) but if it is a scientific gentleman, who wishes the use of it for some months, I might be willing to lend him it against receipt.

At the same time I have this opportunity to write I beg to ask if you are acquainted with a gentleman, who interests himself in Genealogy, and who would permit me to address him about some German families.

Dear Sirs!

Your obedient servant,

H. Krebs.

www.ingramcontent.com/pod-product-compliance
Lightning Source LLC
Chambersburg PA
CBHW020236030726
47497CB00009B/3119